ADORABLE FAT GIRL AND THE REUNION

CAN SHE WIN BACK THE ONLY MAN SHE'S EVER LOVED?

BERNICE BLOOM

DEAR READERS

So, MY LOVELY READERS, where were we when we last met?

You will recall that Mary Brown had been on a valiant Six Week Transformation plan in order to lose weight and look her very best for Charlie's 30th birthday party...because Ted was coming and she was still in love with him and wanted him back. The Six Week Transformation wasn't exactly perfect, and she ended up in hospital at one point.

But then, lockdown happened. The party had to be postponed and Mary spent a lot of time eating cake and becoming a minor celebrity while shielding in her flat with Juan. In common with most of us, she started to go a bit mad during lockdown.

But now lockdown has just ended, and it's time for Charlie's party to take place after all. But will Ted come? Will they get back together? Will it all be smooth sailing from here on in… Um… is anything, ever, plane sailing with the lovely Mary Brown?

SHOPPING TIME

"I feel like a caged animal being released into the wild for the first time," I say to Charlie, as I stand on the doorstep looking out in amazement at the whirl of life beyond my front door. She is standing at the end of my path, leaning on the gatepost and shaking her head as I take tentative, tip-toe steps out of my house. I'm doing it mainly for comic effect, but there is a part of me that feels very strange about being able to walk around and meet people. Those heady pre-coronavirus days were a lifetime ago. Can we really all go out again?

It would be a lie to say that I haven't been out at all during lockdown. Readers who have followed my journey will know only too well that, cautiously, looking from left to right as if a coronavirus bug might leap out and attack me, I have been leaving the house to buy cakes and rescue potatoes (don't ask!). But this is different...this is 'out, out' with other people in real shops.

"It feels odd," I say. But Charlie doesn't seem to think it

remotely strange to be free to walk and meet and talk and hug after months in lockdown.

"I'm just thrilled that I can have my birthday party at last," she says, standing back for me so I can walk through the gate and follow her to her car. "I thought I was going to be 31 by the time I had my 30th."

"Me too," I say. "It feels like a hell of a long time since we organised it."

Rather annoyingly, we can't hold the party in the upstairs bar of the posh pub in Richmond that we spent ages finding and booking. Their social distancing policies would mean us only having half the number we originally planned, and paying twice the price. Instead, Charlie's organising a small soiree at home: an intimate gathering for just a few friends. And, bless her, she has included Ted in the number. To date, though, Ted hasn't replied to the re-worked invitation that Charlie sent out changing the date and location of the party, so I don't know for definite whether he's coming.

"Still nothing from Ted?" I ask.

This has become a frequent question.

"No, angel. Sorry. He did say he was coming originally, though, so unless he cancels, I'd expect him to turn up."

"Yes, but if he doesn't know about the venue change, he won't know where to go. He'll be standing in the pub in Richmond all on his own."

"I sent the new invitation to him three times and the last time it had a read receipt on it. He's got it. I imagine he'll be there."

"OK."

Our mission today is to get something to wear. Charlie has rather ruined the drama of the occasion by already ordering something online: a gorgeous, silver-coloured dress which looks iridescent in the pictures. It's the sort of thing that would look utterly terrible on me but will no doubt look fantastic on her super gorgeous size 10 body. She'll look like a mermaid in it. I would look like a hump-back whale. That's just one of the many differences between Charlie and me.

Anyway, because the dress is such an odd colour, she hasn't got anything to wear with it, so she needs to get shoes and a handbag in either silver or white. Me? I need to get everything: dress, shoes, handbag...the lot. I lost loads of weight in anticipation of this party, with my six-week weight loss plan a while back, but then along came lockdown, with all the attendant cake, wine and lack of exercise, and some of it crept back on. The good thing is that I'm still lighter than when Ted last saw me, but perhaps not as light as I would like to have been.

"I'll park in the middle of Kingston, and from there we can go methodically through the shops one by one until we find the perfect outfit," says Charlie with a huge amount of optimism. I think I'll settle for finding any outfit that fits, never mind one that is in any way perfect.

When we step out onto the streets of Kingston, I'm relieved and delighted to see that the shops are busy, but not completely packed. I imagined that the minute people were allowed out of lockdown they would swarm to the shops in uncontrollable numbers and indulge in the sort of spending sprees that would shame the Kardashians. Apparently not.

The first shop we go into is Zara, and we follow the one-way guidelines as we wander around the store. This is my least favourite shop in the universe but Charlie saw some shoes online that she fancied so thought she'd try them on. But now we're here, she can't see them anywhere. She's clutching a picture of them, so she goes off to talk to the manager, leaving me to find myself a dress.

Shall I tell you what my tactic is for finding a dress in Zara? It's finding a dress in size XXL that doesn't look really, really horrible. That's it. I don't worry about shape, colour, design or length. I just need it to be in XXL and not vomit inducing and I'll consider it a real find.

Today I've found a handful that meet the first criteria but which are so far off meeting the second that trying them on is a complete waste of time. But I'm trying them on all the same, just incase they look much, much nice on me than they do on the hanger (this is what's known as insane optimism).

Charlie joins me in the queue for the changing rooms and looks at the clothes in my arms with disdain. "You need some clothes to do DIY in, do you?" she says.

"These are the only ones that have a chance of fitting me. I'm trying these on whether you like it or not."

"OK, OK," she says. "I'll wait out here. I found these shoes by the way - they're fab. I'm so excited."

I look at the pretty, strappy white shoes in her hand and feel a small pang of jealousy. They have elegant high heels and little diamante pieces scattered across the strap. She'll look lovely: I would break my neck if I did three steps in them.

I walk into the tiny changing room with the curtain across that is utterly useless - it has a gap either side - and no amount of pulling it and trying to trap it shut with my handbag seems to work. I resign myself to the fact that anyone walking past will be treated to the size of an enormous bottom in huge white knickers. Lucky them!

I start to slip on the dresses. If one of them is even remotely tight, I'm going to put it to one side and move on. There's no way I'm going to try and squeeze into anything. I did that before, some of you might remember, and I ended up ripping a dress completely. Now I'm older and wiser and will step out of the ring at the first sign of a fight. I slip the first dress on.

"This is so brilliant," I shout out to Charlie. "I mean really brilliant."

"You've found a nice dress?"

"Christ, no. I've found one that fits."

"Oh great. What does it look like?"

"What does it matter what it looks like? It's a Zara dress and it fits. That has never happened before."

"And it looks OK, does it?"

"God - no - it looks terrible. It makes me look like I'm a homeless tramp. It also makes me look slightly unhinged with these odd straps at the back. But I might get it anyway. BECAUSE IT'S A ZARA DRESS. AND IT FITS."

"Let me see," says Charlie, pushing the curtain aside and taking in the sight of me standing there in all my underwhelming glory.

"Brown and khaki are definitely not your colours," she says. "You look like you're after a role in Dad's Army."

"I know - it's awful. But can you take a picture of me, and make it clear that I'm in Zara."

Charlie takes a photo and heads off to look at other dresses for me.

"Take that bloody thing off and come with me," she instructs as she strolls away to search through the racks for any XXLs that might be lingering, undiscovered in the depths of the smalls, extra-smalls and 'so tiny I can't imagine how any human being can be this small' sizes. I step out of the odd flannel creation, and look down at it, admiringly. Such a shame it looks

5

dreadful. I hand it back to the beautiful, dark-haired assistant (honestly where do Zara find so many gorgeous women?), resist the urge to high five her and tell her that it fits me, and join Charlie on a hunt through the rails.

We look long and hard, honestly we do. Then we try Cos because some of their clothing is very over-sized. I can get into some of the clothes there, but - once again - the dresses I can get into look awful. We try H&M without luck, then make a half-hearted attempt at the clothes in Topshop, but that is just silly. Charlie can barely get into the clothes in there and she's about five sizes smaller than me.

"Coffee?" she says.

It seems like the only way.

We sit outside and order two cappuccinos. Charlie orders a cake but I am too scared to. Tomorrow is T-Day. I have to do my best. OK, it's a bit last minute, but every school exam I ever sat was based on being last minute - a sudden burst of work the day before - why change things now?

"Cheers," says Charlie, raising her coffee cup. "Here's to you fitting into a Zara dress AND a Cos dress. It's a very special day."

I know that, as far as achievements go, it's not up there with finding a cure for cancer or walking on the moon, but my weight has always been a real problem for me so I can never find nice clothes. Being able to turn up and slip into a dress at Zara makes me feel wildly happy. Sometimes it's the smallest things in life that give you the biggest smile.

"And tomorrow is your very special day. Are you excited?" I say to Charlie, knocking my coffee cup against hers again.

"More nervous than excited, really. Mum has been great, helping me to set everything up, but it's quite nerve-wracking having the party in my flat. If it was in the pub, like we'd originally planned, they would have had all the responsibility for providing food and booze."

"I know, but it will be so much lovelier in your home. More special."

"Yes, it will be nice. I'll be happy when everyone's there and it's in full swing and we're all having a good time. Then I'll be able to relax."

"Just tell me if you need me to do anything."

"Of course, I will. Is Juan still OK to come over later and help me with the barrels?"

"I'm sure he is, but I'll just call and remind him. He's been meeting up with Gilly for the first time since lockdown. He was really nervous this morning, kind of scared that Gilly would have gone off him, and found someone else."

"Has he not seen him at all in the whole of lockdown."

"Nope. First time today. I'll call him and see how he got on."

Juan does that annoying thing of answering the phone at just that moment when you think it's going to go to the answerphone. "Hi Juan, it's Mary here," I say before hearing his voice. "Oh, you're there…"

"Yes, I'm here, darling, just couldn't get the phone out of my fanny pack quickly enough."

"I hate it when you call it that. Can't you use 'bum bag' instead? That's horrible in its own right, but slightly more tolerable than fanny pack. As a general rule in life, Juan, I'd say that you should avoid using the word 'fanny' in polite company."

Juan is Spanish. His English is perfect because he has been working as a dancer on cruise ships for the past few years, chatting to English and Americans every day, but every so often he says something that makes me draw breath.

"I shall use the word fanny at the end of every sentence if it's going to produce that sort of reaction from you."

"Ha ha. I was just calling because I'm here with Charlie and she wants to check that you're OK to help her with the barrels later."

"Of course I am, fanny."

"Great. I knew you would be, so that brings us on to the main reason I'm calling...I wanted to find out how it went with Gilly."

"Perfect," he says, happily dropping the need to add 'fanny' onto the end of every sentence at the mention of his new boyfriend.

"Is he there now?"

"Yes."

"I'm really glad. And it's all going well."

"So well," he says. "I'll properly update you tonight. Tell Charlie I'll see her at 7. Did you find a nice dress to wear?"

"Nope, nothing. I'm going to have to wear the leggings I wore all lock down. You know - the baggy ones with no elastic in them that you really like."

"No. You will not wear those things. You're not even wearing them round the house, let alone to your best friend's party."

"I'm only joking. I'll have a look around in the morning for an outfit."

"Tomorrow's the day of the party - you need to be styling your hair and tending to your bits and pieces tomorrow...you can't be arsing around with dresses."

"But nothing I've tried on is right. Aaaaah. No. Oh shit, Oh God."

"What's the matter?"

"I've just seen Dawn. Look, Charlie - over there." Charlie's in the middle of a text and by the time she looks up, Dawn is out of sight.

"I'm going after her. Stay here, I'll be back in a minute."

"What's happening?" asks Juan, as Charlie looks at me open-mouthed.

"I'm going to do some investigating. I've just seen Dawn - you know, the woman who Ted has been going out with. I only saw her briefly. I want to see whether she's with.... Oh my God - there she is. She's waiting for someone. I bet it's Ted. Shit. Oh no, she's waiting for the bus. Hang on. No, someone's got off the bus. He's a big guy. Is that Ted? Yes, it's Ted. Oh no. Oh my God."

"Are you sure?" asks Juan. "You could be mistaken."

"I don't know, and now the bus has moved forward and blocked my view. I bet it was Ted. She's still going out with him. This is a disaster."

Juan listens patiently to my ramblings as I try to run across the road to see who she is with behind the bus, but there's so much traffic, I have to wait for the lights to change and by the time I get there, there's no sign of either of them.

I give a large cry, alarming the two pensioners standing next to me, before saying goodbye to Juan and walking back to Charlie, my heart pounding with the mixture of unexpected exercise and the emotional hit of seeing Dawn and Ted together. I've lost the love of my life.

"It was him, wasn't it?" I say to Charlie.

"I don't know, angel. I genuinely didn't see."

"You must have seen. You saw Dawn, didn't you?"

"No, I was looking at my phone. I didn't see anything."

Well you can take it from me. Dawn and Ted are seeing one another; that's why he hasn't responded to the party invitation. He's in love with someone else.

Can we go home now? I feel like I'm going to cry."

MESSY MESSI

❄

Morning comes abruptly, with the shocking sight of Juan and Gilly leaning over me as I open my eyes.

"We have news," says Juan, with a real note of joy in his voice. "Happy news."

"Judging by the noise the two of you were making last night, and the fact that Gilly is still here, I'd guess that one of you is pregnant."

"Ha ha. No. Wrong. Better news."

"Go on, tell me. It's way too early for me to try to guess."

"Ted has replied to the invitation."

I sit up quickly, almost bashing heads with Juan in the process.

"He has? What? My Ted?"

"Yes - your Ted. Charlie phoned just now."

"Oh my God, oh my God, tell me what he said. No, don't tell

me. I can't bear it. He's not coming, is he? No, don't tell me. He's bringing Dawn. Tell me. Oh God, I don't want to know."

"Do you want me to tell you or not?"

"Only if it's good news."

"He's coming."

"Oh wow," I say, then I go quiet. This is great news, of course. The best news, but I'd kind of resigned myself to the fact that he probably wouldn't be there, and it was far less stressful to think about the party when I thought he wouldn't be there for it. And he'll bring Dawn. He's bound to bring Dawn. He was out and about in Kingston yesterday: why would he not bring her?

"I don't have a dress to wear."

This is a serious issue now. Yesterday I was happy to joke around and make light of it. I thought quite seriously that I could wear some sort of baggy dress from the back of my wardrobe, pile on a load of jewellery and tonnes of red lipstick and all would be fine. Not now though. Christ, now it has become a matter of grave importance. I want to look fantastic. I NEED to look fantastic. I can't wear one of my old tunic dresses that he's seen a million times before. I need something that will really wow him.

"Up you get," says Juan. "I know you don't have a dress to wear, so I'm taking charge of making you look fantastic in time for tonight."

I appreciate his intentions, but his offer leaves me a little concerned. To put it bluntly - there is no way on God's sweet earth that I am having Juan choosing my clothes. If you've read any of my previous books, you'll know EXACTLY why I'm so reluctant. The way he dresses is wonderful but extravagant. He likes to be attention-grabbing, wild and artistic. I spend my days in a green uniform at the gardening centre while he wanders around in sequinned trousers, capes and fancy hats. He bases much of his style on what he wore while prancing about on stage, as a dancer. I've seen mankinis, sparkly leotards and feather boas in his room. I'm not going to the party in a leopard skin mankini.

"Mary, are you listening to me? I'm in charge of making you look adorable and wonderful tonight and Ted will not be able to resist you."

"I just want to lie here for a bit," I say. "Can we start moving a bit later."

"Sure," says Juan. "Is everything OK? You seem subdued."

"I'm scared."

"Scared of what?"

"Well, of seeing Ted. Mainly I'm scared of him walking into the party with Dawn and me bursting into tears or trying to beat her up or something. This is Charlie's night and I don't want to make it all about me, but I love Ted so much I'm scared of seeing him in case he doesn't love me back."

I suppose the truth is that in all the time I haven't seen Ted, but have been looking forward to meeting him, I have been able to hope he still likes me. Now I'm about to be confronted by reality, and it might turn out that he has no interest in me at all.

Juan perches on the edge of my bed.

"I don't have a nice dress to wear, and I know you said you'll help me, but I'm really fat and nothing fits, and I don't want to look completely over the top tonight. I just want to look nice."

"I know. But everyone's dressing up for the party. It's the first time any of us have been out properly since lockdown. It's a nice chance to glam up, regardless of whether Ted's there or not. Just trust me, OK. I won't make you wear something over-the-top; you have my word. Stop worrying, get yourself ready and we'll leave in an hour."

"OK."

Juan stands up and heads towards the door.

"Thank you," I shout after him. "You're a really good friend."

"Love you," he says, blowing me a kiss.

The three of us sit on the bus to Richmond. Two of us with black face masks on, and one of us with a fluorescent green one dotted with large jewels. Do you want to guess who is wearing highlighter green? Yep - the guy who is in charge of dressing me for the party tonight. He's insistent that we head into Richmond to go shopping, but I'm sure I'll have less luck there than I did in Kingston. The shops are much posher, and for far thinner people than the ones in Kingston.

Why is that, I wonder? The posher the shops, the thinner the people they cater for. You have to be a size 6 to shop in Channel whereas Tesco's own brand clothing runs up to a size 30. Are all posh people thin? I turn to Juan to ask him what he thinks, as he stands up and announces that we have arrived in Richmond.

"Let's go into some of the really high-end designer boutiques," he says. "We can look at the most flamboyant outfits they have."

"Are you joking?" I say. Can he not see what size I am? "There's no way on earth that I can fit into anything in the fancy shops."

"Yes, I'm joking. We're not going to drag you round the shops, we're going to pamper you. We have booked you a hair and nail appointment. Gilly and I have already sorted out your outfit for tonight. You'll see it later."

"No feathers or sequins."

"Nope."

"No bikinis or sky-high platforms?"

"Nope."

"Something flattering and straightforward. No bizarre angles or wild colours."

"I promise you; you will love the outfit we have for you. Now, come and meet my friend Davido. He owns *Hair by Davido*: he's brilliant. And he won't charge you because I told him what a great friend you are."

"Wow, thanks," I say, walking through the leopard skin-coloured door of Davido's rather fabulous salon.

We all take a seat on the leopard skin banquette (there's a theme to the decor in this place).

"Do you think that Ted will bring her?" I ask.

"It would be really odd if he did," says Juan. "He knows you are going to be there - at your best friend's birthday party. The only reason he's invited is because of you. To bring Dawn with him would be really out of order."

"I'll kill him if he does," says Gilly, looking really angry. "I will; I'll kill him."

"Love you two," I say, with a smile.

Davido comes across the salon floor like Diana Ross walking onto stage. The man has such presence and so much drama about him. I'm immediately drawn in.

"Ah," he says, reaching me and scrunching up my hair in his fingers. "Interesting colour. Did you dye it yourself?"

Cheeky man.

"I had to," I start to explain. "There was nowhere open during lockdown."

"It's too orange. Let's go more Californian blonde, shall we? That will work much better with the dress. Orange will clash."

How does he know which dress I'm wearing?

"Davido has been fully briefed," says Juan.

"Californian blonde sounds lovely."

"Good. I'm glad you agree. First, we will do your eyebrows, then a fake tanning spray, then we will do your hair, then, while the highlights are developing, we will do a lovely manicure and pedicure, then we will style your hair and you will look like an amazing princess."

"Thank you so much," I say to Davido, as he wanders over to the other side of the salon to sprinkle princess magic onto another customer, then I turn to Juan. "Do you think men notice things like eyebrows and highlights? I don't think Ted ever does. I could turn up tonight without eyebrows and I'm not convinced that Ted would notice."

"I always notice everything about a woman's appearance."

"Ah yes, but you're gay. That doesn't count."

"Thanks," he says, looking appalled to have been dismissed. "I don't think many men notice the details, but they notice the overall effect. So they might not notice that you've plucked your eyebrows into the perfect semi-circle, but they will notice that you look nice. It's better to keep some of the mystery about how you achieve it to yourself, in any case, don't you think? They don't have to know how much work is put into it."

While Juan and Gilly go wandering off to see whether they can get us some coffee, I stay on the velvet banquette and look around for magazines.

"Here you go," says a young man, sliding onto the bench next to me. He is terribly cool with mirrored sunglasses, skin-tight jeans and an expensive-looking leather jacket. He hands me the pile of magazines "You might want to wipe them down with hand sanitiser or something. Presumably you're supposed to do that? Don't you think?"

"I'm sure it's fine." I take the pile of magazines from him and treat him to my best smile. "What are you having done?"

He tells me that he wants a messy haircut. "You know - the sort of cut that when I walk into the room people point and say 'messy, messy.'"

"Oh, right. Well, that's interesting."

I'm called over to the far side of the salon, so I leave my new friend who wants his hair to look messy, and trundle over. My eyebrows are shaped using threading, which I've never had before, and is really strange. They look good afterwards but really red and sore.

Then it's time for the fake tan spray which is every bit as dreadful as you might imagine. I'm supposed to stand there in paper knickers but I can't fit into them, so stand in my own, white knickers, knowing they'll end up covered in brown and it will look as if I've had a terrible accident. She makes me lift up my boob so she can spray properly. How awful is that? My breasts are so low hanging that they're getting in the way of the spray tan. That's not a good thing. Eventually, the humiliating ordeal is over, and I have to stand in front of a fan, still wearing nothing but knickers which now look as if I've pooed in them, to dry myself off before getting changed. Do men have to go through this? Do they? You and I both know that they don't.

When I leave the tanning area and sit down to have my nails done, Juan and Gilly arrive with coffees. "Blimey - you look very dark," says Gilly with a smile. "In a good way."

Yeah, right. I look like I fell asleep in the sun...for about a week.

"I have to wash it off tonight before going out, then it will look better, apparently," I say.

"It will look lovely, I'm sure," says the guy in the chair next to me. It's the man from the banquette earlier.

"Thank you. Hey, your hair isn't all messy yet," I say, leaning over to ruffle it aggressively so that it's standing up all over the place.

"What was that for?"

"Helping to make it messy at no extra cost."

"No Messi - the footballer. I want my hair to look like his."

"Oh. Gosh. sorry." I start to pat down his hair so that it looks tidy again, but he pushes my hand off. The day is not going well: My eyebrows are scarlet, my skin is deep brown, my hair is orange and I've just assaulted a man.

"Time to have your locks styled," says Davido. "Follow me."

I smile at messy-hair man who snarls back, and follow Davido...I've never followed anyone so quickly in my life before. What follows after that is a transformation; chunky highlights, fine highlights, sweeping highlights...all sorts of things are going on, while I sit there looking at my chocolate brown face.

"It's lovely," I say, when he's finished and my hair is soft and swishy and full of buttery highlights. My eyebrows are divine and my toenails and fingernails are cherry red.

We jump in an Uber back from Richmond because I can't face sitting on a bus with a weird coloured face, but my hair - my God, my hair has never looked better. I know it sounds arrogant to say this, but the colour is so fab: all sun kissed. Davido is a miracle worker, and until I glanced at the prices on the outside of the shop, I was promising myself that I will always, always see Davido when my hair needs doing. We walk into my flat and I glance in the mirror, just to check that my hair is really as lovely as it looked in the salon. It is. I mean, my face looks a little bit like I've spent the afternoon with my head in a chocolate fountain, but my hair is golden and gorgeous.

Juan rushes into his room and comes back out with a box. Gilly stands next to him, giggling like a toddler.

"You can open this, but you can't touch what's inside until you have washed all the tanning residue off you," he says.

The box has been sent from abroad. I start to open it with the scissors that Juan hands me, until I get to tissue paper.

"OK, I'll open it from here, so you don't get fake tan on it."

He lifts something out of the paper. It's a gorgeous red dress.

"Oh My God."

It's the dress I saw in Italy. The stunning red dress. Do you remember - it was in Bella Bella boutique and I fell head over heels in love with it.

"How did you get it? I mean - gosh Juan - it's the nicest dress in the world. How did you afford it? How? I mean - what's going on?"

"I phoned them," says Gilly. "You know I used to work there, as the fitness adviser to the hotel, well I explained the situation and they all remembered how lovely you are and they sent over the dress as a gift. She says she put some accessories in the box, too. I don't know whether she has."

Juan checks more closely, and fishes out a lovely gold bangle and gold earrings. My nails are red, my hair is blonde and I am tanned, and now I have lovely gold jewellery and the most elegant red dress I've ever seen.

"You two are amazing," I say, a tear slipping down my face, leaving a greasy track in my tan.

"Hey, don't cry. It's all good. You are going to look amazing. Absolutely amazing."

"I love you," I say, as I go to shower away my ridiculous brown colour. "I love you both so much."

PARTY TIME

OK, I'm here. I'm standing in Charlie's sitting room, talking to Juan and acting for all the world like the sort of girl who always parties in a red dress with a Caribbean tan and newly-blonde hair. But inside I'm a wreck. I may be here in body but in spirit I'm elsewhere ...scanning the room, looking for Ted, wondering whether he'll arrive with Dawn and contemplating exactly what I'll do if he does.

"You don't agree?"

"Sorry," I say. I'm not listening at all, just nodding.

"I was saying that I think post-coronavirus lots of people who have got used to working from home won't want to go back to the office. They will want to carry on working from home. I think there will be lots of companies having to make real adjustments."

"Yes, I agree."

"You're miles away."

"I know, sorry. Just worrying, panicking that he'll arrive with Dawn. Or not come, or something."

"Turn around and face me, stop looking at the door."

I turn as instructed and try to focus on Juan as we continue the conversation about life post-Covid. He's right: I suspect that there will be lots of changes in offices around the country, but it feels very alien to me, with my work in a garden and DIY centre. There's no way I could ever work from home.

"I suppose I could sell primroses on the front step or something? Or perhaps have bags of fertiliser for sale."

Now it's Juan's turn to nod and give me an artificial smile.

"Why are you looking like that?"

"Turn round."

I don't know how long Ted has been staring at me for. Seconds, I guess. But as I look at him and he holds my gaze, my head spinning as my whole body lifts up into my throat, it feels like hours. It feels like my whole world is shifting on its axis as I look at this man, a wave of love for him crashing through me. And he keeps looking at me...not staring in an odd, stalkery way, just looking while a half-smile plays on his lips. And I smile too, and it's as if the wave of love I feel for him is being returned in some unspoken way.

Next, he is walking towards me, his hand stuffed into his pocket like he always does when he is nervous. He doesn't take his eyes off me as he walks. If this were a comedy film, he'd trip over because he's not looking where he's going; he's not concentrating on anything but me.

But it's not a comedy film.

It's real life.

It's me and Ted.

"I'll make myself scarce," says Juan. It feels like seconds later that Ted is next to me, leaning down and kissing me on the cheek: "Hello Mary, how are you?"

"I'm fine," I say. "It's lovely to see you."

"It's lovely to see you too. You look amazing."

"Thank you," I say demurely, delighted that I've managed to accept the compliment without blundering into a 'I don't look that great' routine. I am also delighted that Dawn doesn't appear to be with him. I'm just delighted, really. Head over heels and delighted. And really drunk.

"Can I get you a drink?"

I have a large glass of wine on the table next to me, and I've already had about five, so I certainly don't need any more, but I want to make sure he comes straight back to me after going to the bar that Charlie has set up in the kitchen, so I smile and thank him, and tell him I'd love one. He doesn't even have to ask what I want because he knows I always drink white wine. He knows Sauvignon is my favourite. I feel giddy with excitement. Every part of me feels alive. This moment is the beginning of the rest of my life.

I smile as he walks back over to me; he catches my eye and smiles back.

"A brandy and coke for the beautiful lady in red."

I've never drunk brandy and coke in my life.

"I don't drink brandy," I say.

"Oh. I thought you liked brandy and coke?"

"No. Can I just get a glass of wine?"

"Of course, yes. Coming up now," he says.

Who is he buying brandy and coke for? I bet it's bloody Dawn. I always drink wine. What the hell is he playing at? I can feel my happy mood dissolve with the mention of the unfamiliar drink. Ted is the yin to my yan...we work together, we understand each other.…. we battle together. Now he can't even remember what drink I like. It doesn't matter, but it does. It matters because I'm in a high state of anxiety about all this, and I'm close to tears and drunk and I have so much resting on tonight. And I love him; I love him so much.

He returns holding a glass of wine and hands it to me. I feel like crying. How can feelings of elation that were so real and solid a few minutes ago, feelings that swept right through me, filling my head with joy, suddenly disappear like that?

"So, what have you been up to?" he asks.

"Oh, you know, the normal stuff," I say, taking a huge gulp of my wine. "Just working, seeing my friends." All I've really done is think about him, pray for him to come back to me, and dream about tonight and what it will be like to see him. And he can't even remember what I drink.

"And losing a lot of weight," he says. "You look like you've lost tonnes."

"Yes, I have. I'm trying to get myself into shape, you know…"

"Yes, well you look really good" he says. "It's lovely to see you."

"You too," I reply. I want to ask about Dawn but I daren't. He might be heading back to Dawn's tonight after the party for all I know. I'd rather not know, even though I really want to know.

"Work OK?" I ask. I feel flat, empty, and unable to summon up an interesting conversation with him.

I'm all dazed and confused because he obviously doesn't feel as much for me as I do for him. If you love someone you don't forget what they drink. He has replaced me, and can now not even remember what drink I like.

I need to escape for a moment. "I'm just going to check on

Charlie," I say, easing away from him before I start crying or saying something stupid.

He looks really disappointed, but I wander off anyway, and find Charlie in a small circle of laughing, friendly people, reminding each other about some mad moment in the past when they were drunk and reckless.

"Do you remember when we suddenly decided to go to Paris when we were drunk," one of her friends is saying. "We decided to invite the guys at the next table, when we were at that bar near Saint Pancras. They said they'd come. Do you remember, Mary? We all trooped off to get the last train to Paris, got to the station and realised that none of us had our passports on us, so we just went home."

"Thank God we didn't," Charlie was saying, as I looked around, as surreptitiously as I could, for Ted. "Can you imagine arriving in Paris at about two in the morning, having sobered up on the train, with no idea where to stay and no idea how to get back in time for work at 8am."

I smile along with the stories, but I am too drunk and too pissed off with life to engage properly.

"Are you okay?"

"Of course I am," I reply. I don't want to be a burden, I don't want to drag her away from her happy little group of memories, with my miserable tale about Ted not remembering what I drink.

"Absolutely fine. Don't worry about me, honestly no problem at all."

"Come on," she says, linking her arm through mine and leading me off to the corner of the room. Tears start to spill onto my face before we even get there.

"Gosh, you're really upset. I thought you'd be pleased. Ted

made a beeline straight for you and hasn't talked to anyone else all night."

"Yes, I know."

"So, what's the problem?"

"He just offered to get me a drink and brought me a brandy and coke. I've never drunk brandy in my life. He was obviously thinking of someone else. Dawn, presumably. She's the one he thinks of now, not me."

"Hey, Mary, you're being really sensitive about this. He obviously still likes you. I mean OBVIOUSLY. Just go back over there and talk to him."

"OK," I say, because I don't want to take up any more of her time with my miserable thoughts. But I can't go back over and talk to Ted: I feel too shaken with sadness. Instead I walk into the kitchen and refilled my wine glass. Only this time I fill it right to the top. RIGHT TO THE TOP. It's so full that I can't carry it, so I drink a huge gulp off the top, then another huge gulp, then fill it right up again. If there were food around, I'd be eating it. This is how I cope. It's what I do.

I walk back into the sitting room and see that Ted is in a group, talking animatedly. He signals for me to come over, but I don't want to. My head feels like it might explode. I don't want him to have been with anyone else. Is that strange? It's not only that I want him to be with me now, I want him to have pined for me while we were apart. Like I did for him.

I can't get thoughts of Dawn out of my mind. And he obviously can't either, because he'd offered me her drink, and spent all day yesterday in Kingston with her.

I slip away back into the kitchen and sit down at the small table. Six weeks I have been preparing for this. Six bloody weeks. Then lockdown in which we all started to go mad. Why am I being so ridiculously paranoid about it all? I down my drink, stand up, almost fall over, pull myself upright, push my shoulders back and glance at myself in the mirrored surface of the oven. I look good. OK - maybe not good like Cameron Diaz looks good, but better than I have for years. I'm being silly, I know that, but I want everything to be perfect. I take another large sip of my drink and head out of the kitchen. I am going to talk to Ted and tell him how I feel. I may be drunk, but that doesn't matter. Ted and I are always drunk together. I walk confidently towards the kitchen door before tripping awkwardly again, this time on the bottom of my dress. Shit. I steady myself. I can do this. I walk confidently out, into the throng, determined to tell Ted how I really feel.

I don't have to go too far. No sooner have I stepped into the room than I crash into Ted coming straight towards me.

"Oh gosh, Mary. There you are."

"Here I am," I say, standing there like a fool...right in his way.

"I was just going to put this glass down," he says, indicating a half-drunk glass in his hand. For reasons which I cannot fathom, I grab the glass out of his hand and knock back the drink, handing it back to him, then I walk away, into the party.

I guess I think I am being funny. I don't know? Or perhaps it is the action of a woman helplessly in love and unsure whether the feelings she has are in any way reciprocated.

I sit myself down on the edge of the arm of the sofa, and sip my glass.

"Mary?"

I look up to see Ted.

"I'm heading off now," he says.

"What do you mean, you are going. You can't go."

"I have to, I'm off on a boat trip tomorrow. We're leaving

early and there's going to be lots of drinking and carousing," he says, with a soft smile.

I don't reply. I can't. I'm too busy clinging onto the edge of the sofa and fighting to stay upright.

"We're doing a gentle trip down the river tomorrow, then back to Thames Ditton in the evening, to moor right outside The Albany and have many, many drinks."

I still don't say anything. He's obviously going on the boat trip with Dawn. I don't trust myself to speak.

"After that we're going off for two days. Should be nice."

"With Dawn?" I ask. "Drinking brandy and coke and talking about me and how you don't love me anymore? Well - enjoy yourself."

"No, Mary. Not with D…"

"What on earth do you see in that woman? Have you seen the state of her? She is really fat and really ugly. You've got to admit, Ted. I do I look a lot better than her."

Ted looks stunned.

"Mary, you look lovely. I'm not going out with Dawn tonight or tomorrow night or any night. But you must know me well enough by now to know that I don't go out with people because of the way that they look. And, to be honest, if I want to go out with Dawn, I'll go out with Dawn no one is going to stop me."

I am drunk, confused, and I know I need to shut up. So I do.

Ted starts to walk away.

"Ted, please come back."

"It's lovely to see Mary, but I've got to go now. And –to repeat – you look lovely. I hope you find someone who is worthy of you."

THE MORNING AFTER

"Morning," says Juan, sitting on the edge of my bed. "How are you feeling?"

"Oh shit. Oh God, Oh God, Oh God."

Juan hands me a glass of water.

"I'm just so angry with myself."

"Don't be silly. It's all cleared up now."

"No, it's not. nothing is cleared up; my life is a mess. I'm a complete idiot."

"I promise it's cleared up. I did it myself, with my own fair hands."

"Cleared up what? I'm confused. What are you talking about?"

"The sick."

"OH GOD. I was sick? This is a nightmare."

"Yep, 'fraid so. You were sick all over the sink last night. Don't you remember? At least you made it to the kitchen."

"I'm so sorry. Really sorry. And that wasn't even what I was 'Oh God-ing' about. Shit, I'm really sorry."

"You were in quite a state."

"I made a complete fool of myself, was sick and ruined any chances of getting back with Ted - all in one night. I'm an idiot."

"Come on, tell me what happened?"

"I just turned on Ted for no reason. I got all upset."

"Start right from the beginning. When he first walked in you two seemed to attract one another like magnets. What happened?"

I explain the whole sad tale to Juan...how he bought me the wrong drink and I became convinced that it was Dawn's drink and it all went downhill from there.

"Well it probably wasn't a good idea for us to drink quite as much before we went out, but you seemed OK when we arrived at the party."

"I drank a lot after that, and I was so nervous about seeing Ted. I've had months of thinking about him, wanting to be with him...it was such a dramatic moment finally to see him, and it hit me like a train when I realised that he might not have been feeling the same."

"But you don't know any of this, angel. You're making a lot of assumptions. Perhaps he brought you the wrong drink because he was really nervous. Perhaps he thought about you every day since you last met. You don't know. What you are doing my lovely is catastrophising."

"Go on..."

"Well, it's when you think of the worst possible interpretation of a situation even though you can't possibly know. You're doing it to protect yourself. People who've been hurt in the past do it to avoid getting hurt again. So, if you think of the worst possible outcome and focus on that then you can't be hurt by the outcome, because you've already mentally prepared yourself for the worst thing. It's very damaging though, as you have seen. And it's not fair. You're judging Ted on a little slip-up he made and making yourself believe he can't possibly love you and must be in love with someone else. There's no logic to these assumptions."

"Yes."

"Can you see that he might just have brought you the drink by mistake…no bad intentions, no links to other women - just a guy in front of a girl he loves messing up under pressure. It wouldn't be the first time that had happened."

"Oh no, Juan," I say, burying my head into my hands as he reaches over to comfort me.

"You just have to call him and talk to him properly."

"He's obviously not interested in me, why would I talk to him?"

"You're doing it again, Mary. What makes you think he's not interested you? I saw the way he looked at you, he likes you, but he probably doesn't understand why you suddenly turned on him."

"What about Dawn?"

"I don't think he is going out with Dawn. He might have been on a few dates with her at some stage - who knows? All we know is that he turned up without her and spent the whole evening talking to you, and looking at you like he was obsessed with you. Can't you just take the positives out of it and use this as a reason to call him and try and arrange to see him."

"I wish I could just press rewind and do last night again."

"Phone him. Nothing is irredeemable. Worse things than

that go on in relationships all the time. The most important thing has to be Ted knowing that you still want to be with him."

I nod as Juan speaks. He is absolutely right. But ring him? After everything I said to him last night. "I'll call him when I'm sober. Fancy breakfast?"

Juan and I decide to jump on the bus into Kingston, and walk along the river until we find a little café on the water's edge. Juan immediately orders a full English while I think I'd better play it a bit safer after last night's performance: I go for porridge and a huge bowl of fruit salad. We sit there, looking out across the water, as I try to remember everything Ted said the night before about his boat trip. They were starting from Kingston, though they would be long gone by now because I know he said they had a very early start. Then they would return to Thames Ditton later, and would be at The Albany, the lovely pub right on the river.

As Juan and I sit there in silence, watching the boats go past, you already know what I am thinking, don't you? This evening I will go along the river and try to find him, bump into him, stumble across his boat or something.

"So?" says Juan. "Are you going to call him?"

"Yes, this evening," I say. I don't want to share with him the news that I am going to track him down like in that programme 'Hunted' for fear that he will try to put me off, or even want to come with me. This is something I need to do. And I need to do it by myself.

"Shall we head back," I say. I have plans to make, maps to find, social media to stalk...a large and lovely man to find.

. . .

The first thing I establish, back in the War Room (my bedroom) is that I have no real idea about the timings of the boat trip, what sort of boat it is, how many people are on it, or what this is all about. I don't want to do the whole catastrophizing thing that Juan accuses me of, but it could be a romantic trip with Dawn for all I know.

Facebook is my first port of call, mainly because when I stalked him early on in our relationship, that's where I discovered him posting most frequently. You will remember that it didn't work particularly well that time; I tracked him to a party that he wasn't actually at, and ended up in the back of all the photos taken, which confused the hell out of Ted who could not for the life of him work out why I would be at the party with all his friends. But never mind that. This time it will definitely work.

I open his page but he's posted nothing new. Damn. What do I do now? I call up his friends list, hoping to recognise some of the names on there...I've met a few of his close friends, and I imagine that if he's going away with a group, it will be with them.

I click on Andrew Harper's profile - nothing.

James Henderson - nothing either. Blimey, these guys don't go on Facebook much. Henry Richmond - yes - bingo. His Facebook update says that he's going away for a couple of days before he comes back in time for the reopening of Shambles. Oh, that's good news: Shambles is a fab bar on Hampton Court High Street. It's brilliant. We used to go there all the time, but it shut for refurbishment. Glad it's going to open again soon.

Anyway, where were we...what else does he say? Nothing. Just that he's going away for a couple of days. Bugger. All the chat under the comment is about the reopening of Shambles...nothing about his trip.

I realise I'm going to have to fly by the seat of my pants on this one...luckily, I have very large pants!

I check the bus timings and decide that I will head to Thames Ditton late afternoon/early evening. There's a bus that leaves from outside my house at 4.45pm and gets there at 5pm. That's the one I'll be on. I mark it in my secret notebook in blood (that last bit is not true).

I tell Juan that I'm popping out for a walk, and, at 4.40pm, I close the front door behind me and head off on the R68 bus to Surbiton via Thames Ditton, on my James Bond-style mission.

Once I'm in Thames Ditton I realise that my planning stops here. Clearly, they are on a boat, and boats go on water (notice the scientific level of analysis), so I go to the edge of the river and wander to where boats are moored. I don't know whether their boat is here already or coming later. I might have a wander along the river and see whether I can see any signs. I don't know what signs I'm looking for, to be honest. Perhaps Ted's shoes lying on the river bank or something...anything.

There are six boats, the first two boats look like they belong to families: children's bikes litter the towpath next to them and teddy bears peer out from the windows. Then there is a rather sleek-looking boat that (forgive me) I could never imagine Ted being on, then two boats in a row that are occupied by older people who sit out on the decks chatting to one another. Then...another boat. It's a bit rough around the edges and not as clean as the others. In short, it looks exactly like the sort of boat that a group of blokes would use for a booze cruise. I peer in and it looks empty, which means they are probably in the pub already, or taking a nice stroll along the river. From the front I can see jackets piled up just inside the glass door. One of them looks like Ted's coat. It's navy but with a mustard-coloured lining. Is that mustard? Is it lining, or another coat lying on top of it? It's hard to see. I need to get a little closer to investigate.

Along the edge of the river bank, separating me from the boats is a thick chain slung between concrete bollards. Presumably it is designed to stop people from getting too close to the water and falling in? Or perhaps it's to stop people from cycling bikes onto boats. Anyway, it's not going to stop me. I step over the chain, keeping my eyes peeled and looking around lest Ted should appear. If I see him, I'll have to scarper. I can't think of a reasonable explanation for why I'd be peering through his windows, so running away will be the only option. Sadly, it turns out my attention is focused far too much on looking out for Ted, and not enough on stepping over the chain, as I go flying over it, and land with a giant heap on the front of the boat. The whole thing shakes and creaks. Shit. I clamber onto my feet - not an easy task on a boat that is rocking in the water - and take a step across the deck. God, my shin hurts. I peer in the window. I think it's Ted's coat.

Then there's a creak as someone opens the door, so without waiting to examine the coat any further, I lurch across the deck.

"What do you want?" says the man on the boat. It's not Ted, I'm relieved to see, but it looks a lot like Henry Richmond. I've only met him once through Ted, but I've seen him in Shambles over the years. He works behind the bar there. I have a feeling his parents own the place.

"I'm so sorry, wrong boat," I say, leaping down, back onto the grass, and scrabbling to my feet. "I'm really, really sorry."

With that I run as fast as my legs will take me, racing into the pub, and straight into the ladies to repair my dishevelled appearance.

I pull my makeup out of my bag and start to transform myself into a human again. Then I wander back into the bar and sit down to read my magazines and my book, knowing that Ted will most likely come in later. I've found myself a small table in a central place so that I can see immediately if Ted comes in. Then I pull out my magazine and started reading all the latest celebrity gossip. My shin aches but at least I'm safe and out of harm's way.

I finish my drink, and try to convince myself not to have a second one. Last night's drinking marathon has left me aching from inside out, but the taste of that first glass of wine has washed away all the discomfort and bad memories and left me with a gentle glow that I want to ignite further. Surely one more wine and soda is OK? Also, maybe a bite to eat? I'm making a real night of this. Another glass of wine, a packet of cheese and onion crisps and some of those lovely chilli nuts, and I sit back down with my little picnic.

It's probably been about an hour when I felt a gentle tap on my shoulder and look up to see Ted and three other men standing next to me.

"I didn't know you came here?" says Ted.

I smile at him in the most gorgeous way I know and shrug my shoulders. "It was such a beautiful evening, I thought I'd come for a walk down the river and then stopped off for a glass of wine. What are you doing here? Didn't you say you are going away with the boys?"

"Oh sorry, yes – I thought I explained yesterday – we are doing a trial run up and down the river today, then heading off tomorrow morning. This is Tom, this is Simon, and this is Matt."

I shake hands with the three men, and Ted asks if I mind them joining me.

"Of course not."

"Can I get you a drink?" he asks. "Wine and soda?"

"Thanks, Ted, that would be great."

HELLO, SAILOR

❄

The three guys sit down next to me while Ted goes up to the bar to order the drinks; I excuse myself and walk up to stand next to him.

"I'm really glad I bumped into you," I say.

"I'm glad you bumped into me. too."

"I am mortified about last night. Seeing you there threw me a little bit. Look...I had too much to drink and it all just got really silly. I'm sorry about everything. I just don't know what came over me."

"Don't worry," he says. "It was really hard seeing you last night as well. It was so long since we last saw one another. I didn't know how to act around you. I shouldn't have gone. It was your best friend's birthday. I had no right to be there. I can see why you got angry with me."

"I wasn't angry with you; I was angry with myself...and very drunk."

"No harm done. I'm glad we've seen one another today. The

Gods must be smiling in our direction to have us meet up like this."

"Yes," I say. He doesn't need to know that this entire thing was planned and based on considerable stalking, a dramatic fall onto the boat and an hour sitting here reading Cosmopolitan.

"Are you seeing anyone at the moment?" he says.

"What? You mean like a boyfriend? No, no I'm not," I say in what I hope to be considered a nonchalant, light and breezy manner.

"I saw that you were going out with all these other guys and having a great time without me. I didn't know whether you were still seeing them."

"No, I wasn't. I only went online dating because Juan and Charlie made me. It wasn't a bundle of laughs, I promise you. And the whole thing just taught me that I don't want anyone else."

"I also wondered whether you and Dave had got together, you know - after the videos of you in lockdown?"

"Err...no: I'm not with Dave, and never will be. How about you and Dawn?"

"Never have been, never will be."

"But didn't I see you in Kingston with her a few days ago?"

"Nope. Not me. I've been working like mad recently."

"Oh, right."

"So, we are friends?" he says.

"Of course."

He gives me a big hug and holds onto me a little bit longer than one might if one were just a friend. That pleases me more than anything.

"Could you take these drinks and put them on the table?"

Ted hands me three identical drinks. "It's brandy and coke all round with these guys, which makes it a bit easier."

I look up at him and smile. Brandy and cokes all-round, huh? Christ, I had got things all messed up last night, hadn't I?

I hand the drinks out and ask them about the trip, and what boat they'll be travelling on (I don't mention that I think I've just been on it). They explain that they are only going for a day and a night, and will be back the day after tomorrow.

When I look up, Ted is watching me with a smile on his face, he catches my eye and winks. All I want to do now is stay here and drink and chat and get closer to Ted, then I want him to invite me back to his and I want us to be together properly again. But I don't know whether staying here right now and getting drunk is the right thing. In fact, I'm pretty sure that I should leave and not get drunk because - let's be completely honest - getting drunk is never the answer to anything (annoyingly).

This is one of those occasions when I need to talk to Charlie, so I excuse myself and disappear into the loos. "I'm coming to you live from the ladies' toilets at a pub in Thames Ditton," I say.

"Why on God's good earth are you in Thames Ditton standing in the ladies' loo?"

"I'll explain all the details later, but basically - I knew Ted would be here, and I wanted to talk to him, because I really screwed things up last night and I needed to chat to him and make it right again. Now I'm here and were having a great time. He's with his mates and they seem to like me. I don't know what to do."

"Do about what? That sounds perfect."

"So, do I stay here and get drunk with them or should I leave

ADORABLE FAT GIRL AND THE REUNION

and make him miss me. You know all those rules...I don't know what I'm supposed to do?"

"Have you talked to Juan," she asks.

"No, I rang you. I think I need a female point of view."

"Doesn't Juan always say that a man has to be kept waiting, and the more you push things and make yourself available, the more he will back away? I guess on that basis, you should leave him wanting more. Where is he now?"

"He's in the pub, I've sneaked into the ladies."

"I think you should go back there and tell him it was lovely to bump into him but now you've got somewhere to go. Play him a little bit. You need to see whether he'll make the effort to contact you if you walk away."

"Oh God, but that's so old-fashioned, so silly. After everything that Ted and I have been through, shouldn't I let Ted know exactly how I feel?"

"Yes. You should make sure he knows how you feel, then you should back away and see whether he comes after you."

"OK. I'll report back later. Do you fancy coming down to Juan's Pilates classes with me tomorrow? I promised him I'd go and I can't face going on my own."

"Yeah, of course. Text me later and let's make a plan."

I come off the phone and sigh. What I want to go is go in there and drag him home to mine. But I can't: I need to grow up.

So, dear readers, you will be surprised to hear that I do what my lovely friend suggests, and get myself out of there before drinking and shagging become options that are too alluring to resist. I explain to Ted that I need to leave but it's been great to bump into him and I'd like to buy everyone a drink before going. They all say "no" of course, and try to insist on buying me one before I go, but I remain strong in the face of temptation.

"I need to get back but so lovely to meet you."

Ted comes over and gives me the most enormous hug.

"I'm so glad I saw you, Ted. You look great, by the way. Really well."

"You too," he says and I can see that he means it. I can feel that he really doesn't want me to leave

"Bye everyone," I say, as I spin round to sashay off out of the pub.

You've got to agree - I'm playing a blinder here, aren't I? I've said everything I want to say to him and now I'm leaving him wanting more. Perfect.

Well, almost perfect...until I spin round and go careering straight into Henry; the man who I scared half to death a couple of hours ago by leaping onto the back of his boat.

Oh shit.

"Ah - it's the boat jumper," he says, smiling down at me. He's huge...I never realised quite how tall he was. He must be about 6'6".

"This lady just jumped on our boat."

"No, this is Mary," said Ted. "You remember, Henry - I've mentioned Mary to you loads of times."

"Yes, but it's also the woman who was on our boat earlier. She gave me such a bloody fright, I almost ended up thumping her."

"Ha ha. Bye again, everyone," I say, as I walk at high speed out of the pub, and down the river bank, determined to get away from the pub before my inquisitor can drag me back and further insist that I am the vagrant who tried to board his boat.

I charge along, swinging my arms like every physical

training instructor tells you to, until I am clean away and heading towards the centre of Thames Ditton where I know I can get a bus home.

As I wait at the bus stop, my phone rings. It's Juan.

"Darling, tell me everything, I've just spoken to Charlie, I understand you found your man, and you want to know whether you're allowed to sleep with him."

"Ha ha. Yes, I did, not only did I find him, I was able to apologise to him for last night, and have a drink with him and behave in a very civilised way. I even managed to leave while he still wanted more. He was desperate for me to stay, Juan, but I left. I was very calm, very sophisticated and very alluring. You would be very proud of me."

"So, all in all an immaculate performance."

"Kind of peerless," I reply. "Well, my interactions with Ted were, though I had a bit of an issue with the owner of a boat that I fell onto. I'll tell you more when I get home, but I think I just about got away with it."

TRAIN ANNOUNCEMENTS

❄

I am up early the next morning, pretending that I want to go to Pilates with Juan, when all I want to do is lie in my bedroom thinking about Ted. Sadly, because I'm 30, and not 14, mooning around and listening to love songs while thinking about Ted isn't an option...so I get into the shower, put love songs on, and think about him in there instead.

You must be clean by now," shouts Juan, gently knocking on the door. "I need to get a shower before we go."

I step out of the water, and switch off Lionel Richie who is telling me that I am once, twice, three times a lady, and dart off to my bedroom to get changed. I don't have an abundance of clothing that is suitable for Pilates. No lycra leggings or crop tops or anything like that. Instead I put on my daily non-work uniform of T-shirt and tracksuit bottoms and head to the kitchen to make myself some breakfast.

"Don't eat too much, will you," says Juan. "It can be hard work doing Pilates on a full stomach."

"Another reason to hate PILATES," I say, while taking a huge bite out of toast covered with peanut butter. I'll only have one piece, and take an apple and a banana with me, and that counts as not having a full stomach in anyone's book.

"This should be fun today," says Juan, joining me in the kitchen to make himself a gruesome-looking protein shake. It reminds me of the time when I tried to go on a diet, one of many diets I have tried over the years, this one involved eating nothing but green shakes, they made me so ill that I was sick and bright, livid green liquid came out of me. It's been peanut butter on toast for me all the way, ever since.

The doorbell goes, quickly followed by the sound of Charlie letting herself into the flat. She's got a key, but is always courteous about knocking first, just in case we are up to no good. Sadly, we are very rarely up to no good in here.

"Let's go," says Juan. "The bus goes in 10 minutes."

"Don't be daft," says Charlie. "I'll drive us there, that will be much nicer."

"Oh, you are a darling," says Juan, giving her a big hug. "I'm really worried about being late. I know where you can park."

So off we go then, the four of us packed into Charlie's little mini as we wind our way through the streets of Cobham and over to Thames Ditton. It's very 'olde worlde' sort of place, with a lovely little old-fashioned post office and chemist, like a country village, but on the river and only 20 minutes from Wimbledon. I love this part of the world. I feel so lucky to live here.

"Right there," says Juan, who has been successfully directing

Charlie and now has pointed out the sneaky free parking spaces round the back of the health and fitness studio.

Once she's safely ensconced in her parking place, Juan and Gilly head off into the studios, with Charlie and me close behind.

"There are four classes this morning: beginners to start with, then Pilates on the ball, Pilates with a band, and yogalates - that's a mixture of Pilates and yoga. I don't really approve of mixing Pilates and yoga together, but they are paying me extra to run it so I said 'yes'."

"Ahhh...so your Pilates morals can easily be bought then?"

"Absolutely, honey," he replies. "Everything about me can be easily bought."

I give him a big hug because I like it when he is being daft and silly. He tends to be very serious when talking about Pilates. He sees it as the route to all that is good, proper and wonderful in the world. He genuinely thinks he changes lives and that we would all be better people if we did more of it.

"You go and get yourself a coffee or something, and I'll go and sign in and get ready for the class. We're in studio two. Don't be late for the first class."

"Oh, I can't actually do the class - I have to take the car in to get its MOT," says Charlie. "I just came along to support you."

I feel my heart lift with joy at this news. "Yes, I'm going to go with Charlie and we'll see you back here later."

"Oh, OK. We'll see you later."

"You don't have to come with me," says Charlie. "Stay and do Pilates."

"Mate, I would genuinely rather go with you to get the car MOT-ed than put myself through agony in a sweaty room full of sweaty people. Having said that, this is a lovely place, isn't it?"

"Yes - very swish."

I hadn't expected *Thames Pilates* to be anywhere near as elegant as it is. It is new and all clean and shiny. White walls with all these beautiful works of art on them. Ballet dancers and gymnasts posed in weird positions to display their flexibility...legs wrapped around the backs of their necks or doing back bends and poking their heads out from in between their legs. All very unnerving and deeply unnatural.

In the cafe there are inspirational quotes all over the wall: *"All progress takes place outside the comfort zone." "The only place where success comes before work is in the dictionary."* You know the sort of thing.

Charlie and I coo with delight when we see they are selling proper coffee made with coffee beans and milk. There are a million types available, of course, including oat milk, decaffeinated, low fat and virgin's toenails or something, but also proper coffee. Perfect.

"I'm still feeling concerned, you know."

"About what?"

"Whether Ted now thinks I'm mad. You know, with me jumping on the boat and Henry seeing me. Ted hasn't been in touch at all."

"You wouldn't expect him to though, would you? He's away with the guys, they were probably hammered by 9am this morning. And I wouldn't worry too much about this Henry guy. Ted likes you. We know he's not seeing Dawn. It's just a matter of time now before the two of you are back together and you're smiling like you used to."

"I hope so. I could really have done without Henry arriving in the bar."

"Kind of funny though…"

"Yeah, I guess. Also completely ridiculous."

"Come on, let's go and drop this car off, then we can come back here and have more of this fine coffee."

We drive to the garage in Wimbledon and leave the car with three mechanics who look entirely irresponsible, before heading to the station to get a train back to the gym. We stand on the crowded platform and I look across at all the people fighting to get on and off trains. It's mostly men, in their safe uniforms of suits and ties, heading into offices in central London. I watch them all and wonder. Would I like to do that? I'm very critical of my job in the gardening and DIY centre, and I make fun of the silly uniform I have to wear, but I do prefer to be working locally, and messing around with plants all day, than getting on trains and tubes and fighting my way into central London. It must be quite glamorous, though, having an office in town and going to executive lunches and important meetings.

"Do you ever wish you worked in town?" I ask Charlie.

"No. I don't think I'd want to commute every day, but it must be fun sometimes. Imagine if we were in really important jobs, both of us with fancy offices, meeting for lunch and having loads of money."

"Yeah, I think I'd really like that. I might start looking around for a different job, or maybe do a course or something? What do you think?"

"That's a great idea. You've been at Foster's for ages, and you know you could do much better, and earn more money."

"Yes - let's make a pact - we're both going to get better jobs."

"Deal."

We shake hands and give each other a hug. I feel happy and lighter for having made the decision to try and make a little more of myself. I know I can do different things with my life, I just lack confidence after everything that's happened to me.

As I'm standing there, contemplating how I'd change the world if I were in charge of it, a guard walks past us and up to a small phone on the wall. He announces that the next train is the 10.27 train to Hampton Court, calling at Thames Ditton.

"Our train," says Charlie, unnecessarily.

The guard walks away to the other side of the platform, with his whistle in his mouth and - I'll be frank, lovely readers - I do something completely ridiculous. I smile at Charlie and walk over to the phone on the wall. The train arrives and opens its doors and people tumble out.

"This is the 10.27 train to Hampton Court. This is a women-only train. Only women are permitted to travel on this train," I announce.

I look up at the platform, where women are gingerly getting on the train and men are looking around, unsure.

A man in a blue suit and red tie steps onto the train.

"Gentleman entering the train in carriage seven, please step down. This is a women-only train."

The man looks round.

"Yes - you with the blue suit and red tie. Off the train please."

Women all step onto the train and men stay where they are. It's the funniest thing ever. No one knows quite what to do. Then I see the guard running across the platform towards me. "Hey, put the phone down," he is shouting. I put the receiver back and run to jump on the train.

"I know who you are. The police will be notified," he shouts, and I have a small panic. I only meant to have some harmless fun. What if he calls the police?

"I'm going to jail," I say to Charlie, but she's not able to answer me, she's laughing so hard she can barely breath, while the guard's voice booms across the platform. Next to us two men are discussing whether they should be on the train, or whether this is for females only.

"This train is for everyone," the guard is saying, as it starts to pull out of the station. "All passengers may travel on this train, not just women. This train is for men too."

THREE'S A CROWD

❄

Charlie and I are regaling Juan and Gilly with the story of my madness on platform eight as the phone rings from somewhere in the deepest recesses of my handbag. I just sit there, looking at Juan, Gilly and Charlie.

"Aren't you going to answer it?"

"Nope," I say. "I think we all know who will be on the phone: some sneering suit from British rail objecting to my little prank."

"It won't be the bloke from British Rail, don't be ridiculous. He was only winding you up."

"I bet it is him. I've got previous for this sort of thing. Remember when I put my name down as a joke to win a £5k sketch in a blind auction, I won the damn thing. It's hanging in my flat now, in case you hadn't realised."

"Yes, that was a particularly ridiculous moment," says Charlie. "But – you never know – one day that print could be worth tens of thousands, and you'll be able to retire to a yacht in the Caribbean on the back of it."

"Yes, it could happen," I say, shrugging to indicate how entirely unlikely this is.

In the meantime, the phone in my handbag rings again.

"For God sake answer it, it's probably just your mum."

Oh actually, that's probably not a bad shout. I haven't spoken to mum for a few days, and she does worry if I'm not in constant contact with her. I push my hand into my bag and put out my phone, I look at the screen and scream like I've just seen something terrifying.

"It's Ted."

All the faces round the table have raised eyebrows, as I answer the phone and move away to the other side of the cafe.

"Hi Ted," I say.

"Oh, Mary, you are there. How are you?"

"I'm okay. Just having a coffee with Charlie, Gilly and Juan. How are things with you? How was the boat trip?"

"Honestly, it was absolutely brilliant. You and I should do something like it; it was so great. Just beautiful to be able to while away the day sitting on the boat watching the world go by, waving at people on the towpath. It was very relaxing."

"Sounds lovely."

"Look, Mary, I'm at work at the moment, so it's difficult to talk properly, but I just wondered... Do you fancy meeting up for a drink, maybe a bite to eat, later in the week?"

"Sure," I say, hoping I sound nonchalant. "I could do Friday?"

That's tomorrow night. I can manage to wait till then.

"Okay, Friday it is then. I will make a plan and I'll pick you up at eight. How does that sound?"

"That sounds lovely. Looking forward to it," I say, while

looking over at the table where Gilly, Charlie and Juan are staring at me wide eyed and eager for some sort of information.

"I'll see you then. If there's any problem, or you can't make it for any reason, just send me a text," he says.

I walk back to join the others, thinking that even if war breaks out, both my legs fall off, or I end up in jail, I will still make Friday's date.

"Everything okay?" asks Charlie with a smile. She can clearly see from my face that everything is perfectly okay.

"He asked me out on a date on Friday night."

"What did you say?" says Gilly.

"I said yes, of course. Now I just have to work out what I'm going to wear."

"This is the best news ever. Best news EVER. Shall I come back to yours and we can go through your wardrobe and find something lovely?" says Charlie.

"And me too," adds Juan. "I did make you look completely beautiful for the party. Let's style you up again."

"No," I say. "I'm going to stay casual for this. We are just going for a drink locally, it's not a big drama, no styling needed. But since it's now lunchtime I do think we should head back and order those Jamaican roti in for lunch. What do you think?"

All of the heads nod in agreement.

Roti are delicious. Have you ever had one? They are soooo nice. We sit on the floor in a circle for no obvious reason, and make all sorts of mmmm... and ahhhh... sounds as we eat. Then Gilly drops a bombshell.

"I think I overheard something interesting last night," he

says. It turns out he's not really doing justice to the word interesting, because what he overheard is unbelievable.

"I was putting the bins out and I heard Dave downstairs discussing with this girl he's been seeing about meeting another girl in a pub to see whether they should have a threesome."

See. Proper gossip, isn't it! I know that sort of thing happens in *Sex in the City*, but really and truly, in real life, have you ever heard of anything so ridiculous?

"Go on..." I say to Gilly.

"Dave saw me and realised I'd overheard so asked me not to tell anyone, but I think he was well aware that I would.

"They are meeting her in Shambles tonight. He says he put some sort of advert on some internet site asking for a young female to join them. She replied and now they get to meet her for the first time at 8 o'clock."

"You know what we should do, don't you? We should go down there, and see what's going on."

"Oh God yes. We absolutely should," I say, not realising that I'm about to walk into Shambles and have the shock of my life. I mean: A REAL SHOCK.

SHAMBLES IN SHAMBLES

❄

It's so nice to be back in Shambles again. This is the place that Charlie and I used to come to when we were younger, I remember celebrating my 18th birthday in here. The guys behind the bar had a small panic when they realised I was celebrating my 18th, considering I'd been in there so often over the years that they all knew my name. I've met just about every boyfriend I've ever had in this place.Shambles was always the best place to meet.

I still remember the joy I felt when they started playing music on Sunday nights, and everyone was up dancing to ABBA and Madonna, it was wonderful. All this old-fashioned music blaring out, and loads of us dancing around, trying to forget the hangover that had been threatening to kill us all day.

It's been shut for refurbishment forever but happily, like so many of these places that shut for weeks for refurbishment, it has reopened and really doesn't look that different. Which I'm glad about. There are new lights, freshly painted walls and funky pictures and stuff, but it's still the same old Shambles that we all adore.

We decamp to a corner table and I proceed to tell Juan and Gilly a few tour tales about our Shambles shenanigans over the years, before the conversation inevitably moves onto the subject of Dave.

"So, remind us...Dave is coming here with a girl he's been seeing to discuss a threesome."

"If they fancy the girl who turns up," says Gilly. "Apparently Dave is up for it, whatever she looks like, but the girl he's been seeing - I can't remember her name - she wants to make sure she's attracted to the woman before anything happens."

I look at Charlie and we both smile. This is the greatest amount of fun ever.

"What do you think she will look like?" I say.

"She's bound to be around 20, skinny, with long wavy hair. All of his women look the same: like Barbie dolls."

"Dave's gonna freak when he sees us all sitting here," I say.

"I know. And he'll realise that I've told you," says Gilly. "We need to bury ourselves in the corner. If he sees us, he'll know we're watching him."

"I'll go to the bar now, and get more drinks," says Juan. "Then we can stay put and just watch from a safe distance."

You see - we're treating this with all the seriousness it deserves.

"I'll come with you," I offer. "Let's split the round...get a couple of bottles of wine to keep us going."

We walk up to the bar, cautiously, looking left and right to make sure Dave isn't here anywhere. Then I see him.

"Oh My God," I say to Juan. "Look who it is."

"Dave? Where?"

"No, not Dave - that's Ted. Sitting right there, with his back to us."

"Oh yes. Go and talk to him."

"No, I don't want to. I'm not wearing my perfect outfit, and I'm seeing him tomorrow night anyway."

"Don't be such an idiot - just go and say 'hi'."

So, I do. I wander up to Ted and touch him lightly on the shoulder.

He turns round and sees me. And he smiles. Well, sort of. He does a rather embarrassed smile like he doesn't really want to see me.

"How are you?" he asks.

He's bright red.

He doesn't stand up and hug me or kiss me on the cheek or invite me to join him.

"I'm OK. Just have a drink with the guys."

"Good, good," he says.

He wants me to go. I can sense that he wants me to leave. He doesn't want to talk to me.

"OK, well - nice to see you," I say, and I turn to go...and find myself face-to-face with Dawn.

"What are you doing here?" I ask.

But I know.

She's with Ted, obviously.

Dawn and I are standing there like cowboys in the Wild West...staring at one another.

"Can I get past you? To my seat. Next to Ted," says Dawn, with a horrible, patronising smile.

"Of course," I say. "He's all yours."

Ted doesn't say anything. I look up at Juan, standing there

with three bottles of wine. "Can we take those back to mine?" I say, trying desperately hard not to cry.

"Of course, angel."

He hands me the bottles and heads over to tell Gilly and Charlie that we are leaving. Then he turns back on his heels. "You giant pig," he snarls at Ted. "Cerdo Extraordinario."

Then he storms over to the others, and through a veil of tears I see them stand and gather their things and head over to me.

"Let's go," says Charlie.

Ted doesn't say a thing.

SHEILA THE HEALER

It's amazing how cathartic it can be to do the dishes REALLY LOUDLY on a Friday morning. We have a dishwasher, but nothing beats stomping around the kitchen and throwing plates, knives and saucepans into a sink of soapy water. I let the water splash up and enjoy the sight of bubbles as they hit the tiles behind the sink and run down them in a watery lather.

There's water all over the floor and I'm so wet I look like I've been bathing in the sink.

"He didn't even comment. Not a word," I say, as a mug crashes into the water. "I see the whole thing with crystal clarity, now. He wants to be with her, not me. Then when I come jigging along into the pub, and he's drunk with all his mates, he thinks I look nice and decides to ask me out. Well, he can forget that."

I keep seeing the look on his face: his eyes widening upon seeing me. The sight of Dawn walking towards us.

I throw the last plate into the sink with such force that it smashes against the mug in there and breaks into pieces.

"For the love of God, woman, will you stop taking it out on the crockery," says Juan, appearing in the kitchen doorway, his face a picture of anxiety and concern, as he looks from me to the smashed plate and the bubbles up the walls and all over the floor.

"I'm pissed off," I say.

"Uh, yeah. Clearly."

"I thought he liked me. I'm such an idiot."

"He does like you, it's obvious he likes you. You just need to talk to him, find out why he was out with Dawn after telling you that nothing was going on between the two of them."

I shrug at him, like an angry schoolgirl.

"There could be a straightforward reason for her being there."

"Yes - very straightforward - because they are going out together."

"No, I mean straightforward as in: they just bumped into one another, they are working together on a project... something like that."

"Have you been speaking to him?" I growl.

"No, of course not. Why would I speak to him?"

"I don't know, but you sound like he does in all the messages he left last night… 'oooo please call me back, there's a very straightforward explanation.'"

"Darling, you have to talk to him."

"No."

"You'd rather smash all our crockery up instead, because that's really going to help you."

"I'm going for a lie down."

ADORABLE FAT GIRL AND THE REUNION

I leave Juan standing in the kitchen, surveying the scene, while I go to my room. I throw half the pile of clothes off my bed onto the floor, leaving the rest of them where they are, as I join them on the duvet. Soon I kick those onto the floor too, leaving loose change, a hairbrush, someone's business card and various knickknacks on the bed. I knock the brush onto the floor, enjoying the sound as it clatters onto the wood.

Then I pick up the card to throw that onto the floor.
But then I look at it.
My world spins on its axis.
Sheila The Healer!
Why the hell hadn't I contacted her before?
She's a woman whose wise words and accurate predictions will guide me seamlessly through this mess.

I went to see her before lockdown and she predicted that I would get back with Ted but that it would take some time. She made other predictions and they all came true. I scrabble around on my desk for the notebook on which I made notes last time. Here it is. Right. What were the predictions?

- **I'll lose some weight and feel better.** Yes, that came true
- **I'll have a surprise visit in the morning.** Yes - that came true too. Gilly turned up the next morning to do fitness training with me. Then Juan and he fell madly in love.
- **I'll get a new job next year.** Oooo...I hope I do.
- **There will be red in my life that I will feel positive about.** Yes. That must be the red dress.

They have all come true. That's incredible when you think

about it. I mean - you could argue that if she can predict the future, she should have predicted the coronavirus or even have hinted that there might be a worldwide health problem on the horizon, but - hey - none of us is perfect.

I pick up my mobile and dial her number, waiting for either the dulcet tones of her grumpy, tv-watching husband or the formal answerphone message, instructing me to ring her on her office phone.

This time, I get neither.

There is no response. Not only does she not answer, but the message machine doesn't click in, so I can't even leave a message for her.

I try again, but the same thing happens. There is only one thing for it - I'll have to go and find her. I grab my coat and flee the flat, heading for the 411 bus to her house.

"Where are you going?" asks Juan, running after me with a mop in his hand. He's clearly decided to tackle the bubbles all over the floor.

"I'll be back soon," I shout. "I owe you one for cleaning up after me."

"Don't go to Dawn's house," he cries. "Whatever you do, don't confront Dawn."

I smile at him as I step onto the bus. As we move forward, he's still shouting and waving his mop. I realise, as soon as I'm on the bus, that I have forgotten my face mask. It's quite busy and I'm not sure whether I'm allowed to sit down next to anyone without it. Certainly no one seems very keen on me sitting next to them from the glares I'm getting, but that could be to do with my size as much as the virus.

I decide to stand, and watch out of the window as the world goes by. It's still funny to see people walking along, shops open and cafes inviting people in after lockdown. I got so used to the empty streets - devoid of cars and people - that it feels like I'm in another country now they're all out and about again. Like I've been dropped into the heart of New York.

My phone bleeps. For some reason I know it's Ted. I think of deleting the message without reading it. I don't want to hear lies. But, Of course, I can't resist it.

"Mary, I love you," he writes. "I'm sorry that everything has got so messed up and I'm sorry you think I was on a date with Dawn last night. I promise you I wasn't. I can explain. Please meet me tonight in Shambles. I'll be there from 9pm. You don't have to stay, but please let me talk to you. Let me explain. Please."

Soon the bus has taken me beyond the bright lights of Kingston and down to the rough estates where Sheila lives. There are children playing outside like the last time I visited, and the usual sprinkling of bikes and scooters across the pavement. I walk up to her door, knock cautiously and wait for the sound of her dog barking. There's no sound of canine activity, just the heavy footsteps of a person walking across the hallway. The door opens a sliver and her husband answers. He's wearing a vest - happily it's not a string vest, but it's revealing enough to show me his man boobs and a colossal amount of body hair sprouting from his shoulders and from under his arms. He looks unshaven and angry, but I get the feeling that he always looks like that.

"Hello, I'm sorry to disturb you, is Sheila there? I tried calling but there's no answer."

"She's not here, love," he says, obviously recognising me from last time we met. "I think she's going to do a reading. She shouldn't be long because she's left Tyson here."

"Thank you," I say, smiling to myself that he's called the dog 'Tyson' - the name he wants for it, while Sheila calls the dog 'Merlin.' - a much more appropriate name for the dog of a mystic.

I know exactly where Sheila will be, once he says she is doing a reading...exactly the same place that she took me: Asda. Sheila loves doing readings in the frozen food section of the local Asda because she is convinced it is built on an ancient burial ground, and enables her to access her spiritual guides more readily. One particular frozen food counter gives her the best results. But while Sheila delights in the fact that spirits roam around the store, the staff are less pleased, and she is chased away by staff as soon as she gets going. Sheila seems to derive an extraordinary amount of pleasure out of the chase. Conversely, the staff at Asda clearly find it all really annoying.

I call an Uber and head to the carpark at the massive Asda. Through the main doors and down towards aisle four I go. I can see exactly where she is by the crowd that has gathered. I linger on the edge, listening to her as she makes predictions and gives gentle warnings and kind thoughts from other realms. It pleases me that the woman she is talking to is being given completely different advice from that which I was given. If Sheila said exactly the same thing again I'd have been sure she just made the whole thing up. She tells the woman that she will be going to go to France, news which seems to excite the woman a great deal. While Sheila scans the cards, the inevitable announcement comes.

"Supervisor to aisle four, please. Supervisor to frozen goods."

Sheila swipes her hand across the top of the freezer and swooshes all the cards into her bag. She is wearing the same elaborate cape as she was wearing last time I saw her as she races out and goes weaving through the crowds with her dramatic cape swinging behind her. She is swiftly followed by the entourage that had gathered to hear the reading, staff from the shop who want to talk to her and me - waddling along behind, shouting her name.

MEN IN SEQUINNED LEOTARDS

"Sheila, it's me – Mary Brown – do you remember? You did my reading for me. You are amazing. Please, please, please can I talk to you."

Sheila hands me her bag and tells me to jump into the passenger seat. As soon as I put my weight onto the seat and lift my feet off the floor, but long before I have closed the door, Sheila is off ...flying out of the car park like a woman possessed.

We pull up in a layby around a mile away.

"What's the matter?" she asks, looking over my shoulder as she speaks to check the management haven't followed her.

"You made predictions about my future and they came true. I desperately need some more help."

"What sort of help?"

"Another reading."

"You need to book."

"Oh please - I'm desperate."

"You want me to do the reading now?"

"Yes please, Sheila. Please."

"It's have to be with the crystal ball. I only have the energy to do tarot readings a day and I've done them both."

"OK, that's fine. Anything. Is the crystal ball like the tarot cards?"

"They are essentially the same. But the crystal ball is a little bit more focused. The tarot gives you general life directions, but we can ask specific questions and get information back from the ball."

"That sounds perfect."

She puts her hand into the bag that is resting on my knees, and pulls out her crystal ball. Pushing down the arm rest between us in the car, she puts the ball onto it. This is my new one with lights and colours to help me interpret all the messages coming through.

She runs her hands over it and throws her head back like she's going into a trance.

"I just want to know whether I'll ever get back with my boyfriend?" I say. "His name's Ted and I love him so much."

She snaps her head back suddenly, like she's abruptly left her trance.

"Dead," she says.

"What do you mean?"

"Dead. Completely dead. There's nothing I can do. I'm sorry."

I am about to burst into tears when she looks me in the eye and shrugs.

"No, no, no," she says. "Not the man you're in love with, I mean the crystal ball is dead. The batteries have run out."

"Oh God, Oh God. I thought you meant that Ted was dead."

And then I can't help myself, it's all too much for me. I burst into tears.

"Why are you crying?" she asks, with rather less sympathy than the whole exchange merits, to be fair. She did just say that Ted was dead.

"Come on, let's go and get some batteries and find out what's in store for you, you sensitive little thing."

She spins the car round, narrowly avoiding an oncoming car, and missing a tree by a fraction of an inch, then zooms off back down the road towards Asda.

"You're not going back to Asda for batteries, surely," I say.

"Yes," she replies. "It's the nearest place."

"I know, but you got chased out of there."

"All part of the fun," she says, parking up and looking at my fearful tear-stained face with dismay. "You really should lighten up a bit. This is what life's about. Anyway, I happen to know with some confidence that nothing bad is going to happen to me in Asda, so we're OK."

She goes to step out of the car but I intervene. "You stay here, I'll go and get the batteries." I jump out of the car and run across the car park before she can stop me. The woman is nuts. Properly bonkers. If I didn't know for sure that she could help me by predicting my future, I'd be staying as far away from her as was humanly possible.

It's not until I am in the queue that I realise I have no idea what batteries it takes.

"Can I have four AA and four AAA batteries?" I ask, it must be one or the other, surely. Then I pay and rush out past the security guard who chased us earlier. He gives me the sort of look you give to someone who you know from somewhere, can't remember where, but know it wasn't good.

Back in the car we establish that none of the batteries will work. It has its own in-built battery that has to be recharged. Sheila lets out a slow whine.

"We could go back to mine?" I suggest. "I'm not that far away."

"But your place might not have the right vibe," she says. "This Asda oozes otherworldliness that allows me to tap into clients' moods and feelings."

"I know. I understand that. But Asda is also a commercial operation, and they aren't very keen on you turning up there and reading fortunes."

"It's all very unreasonable of them. Maybe we should go back to yours and charge the battery, then we could come back here to the reading?"

"Could do that," I say, "Or we could see what the vibe is like at mine and whether you can do the reading there?"

We agreed on this course of action, and I direct Sheila back to my place.

"Nice," she says, admiring the house from the pavement. "Do you own this?"

"No, I just rent the top flat. There's a guy called Dave who lives below me. It's only a small flat, but I love it."

I lead her up the stone steps to the front door.

"I knew that," she says. "I knew about you renting it and about Dave living below. I'm a psychic."

I open the front door for her to step inside. I can hear loud music coming from the sitting room. I sometimes forget that Juan is living with me. I've had so many years of coming back to an empty flat that it takes me by surprise when I hear his music or smell his cooking smells.

But I've never been taken by surprise quite as much as today when I throw open the sitting room door to see Juan and his boyfriend Gilly dancing around to 80s music, dressed in matching sequinned leotards.

They continue to dance for a while, unaware that they are being observed. Gilly shaking his butt cheeks in a leotard which clearly belongs to Juan. It's a good couple of sizes too small for him, meaning he is hanging out and bulging out all over the place. I look at Sheila whose eyes look as if they might burst out of her face. Well, I bet you didn't predict this, did you, mighty Sheila?

Finally, Juan spots us, stops mid twerk, and smiles.

"Hi," he says without a hint of embarrassment. "Are you feeling a bit better now? I cleaned all the mess in the kitchen and now we're having a rather drunken day. Fancy joining in?"

"We probably won't join in, but thanks for the invitation. Nice to see you, Gilly," I say.

Gilly has none of the wild confidence that Juan was blessed with. He stops dancing as soon as he sees us and plunges to the floor, using the sofa as a shield. We look from Juan, still dancing, to the sofa behind which Gilly lays while Kylie's greatest hits continue to belt out in the background.

"Come on, let's all dance," says Juan.

"We haven't really got time," I say. "We've got things to do."

But Sheila seems completely entranced, watching them with alarming intensity.

"It is all Dave's fault," says Juan. I hear the slurring in his voice that I hadn't noticed before, and realise that yes they are actually very, very drunk.

"How is it Dave's fault?"

"He came up to see you, and then when you weren't here, he stayed and drank all the booze in the place. We asked him about the threesome thing last night but he said he made it up to shock Gilly."

"I wasn't shocked," says Gilly, still behind the sofa.

"Where is he now?"

"He's gone down to his flat to get some vodka and wine. He should be back in a minute."

There is a loud knock that unmistakably belongs to Dave from downstairs. I swing the door open to the most unbelievable insight in the history of the world. I don't know whether you have a sense of just how handsome Dave is. If you've read my previous books, you'll know that he is a standout beauty of a man, with a chiselled jaw, bright green eyes and lovely long lashes. He is always stubbly, always slightly dishevelled in the manliest way imaginable and normally dressed casually in jeans and a T-shirt or gym shorts that he's thrown on to go out and exercise. When he's going out somewhere smart, he wears a white shirt with his jeans and just looks amazing. Today? Ladies, today he is wearing one of Juan's sparkly leotards. How many leotards does that man have?

"Hello gorgeous," says Dave, leaning in to kiss me on the cheek. I didn't realise quite how hairy he is, he has the body of a bear.

"What the hell on earth are you wearing?" I ask, as he wanders into the house, giving us a sight of his magnificent backside, where the leotard, a good two sizes too small, has ridden up.

"Well hello," says Sheila. "You're a sight for sore eyes."

"This is Dave. He is my neighbour from downstairs, he pops up every now and again, but usually he is fully dressed."

"Yeah, sorry about this. All Juan's fault. We are having a sequin leotard party."

"Can anyone join in?" says Sheila, sidling up next to him and stroking his very hairy shoulder with her ring bedecked hand.

"You have to get a sparkly leotard on if you want to join in," he says, winking at her and prompting her to giggle like a 14-year-old.

"Alternatively, I could just pour you a glass of wine?"

"That would be wonderful," says Sheila.

"Is it a good idea to drink if you're about to do my reading?" I ask her. I don't think she has any idea just how important this reading is to me. "And also, remember you've got the car outside."

This whole scenario is making me feel a little uncomfortable. Sheila pouting in the direction of Dave who is very drunk and wearing a sequinned leotard, along with my wonderful gay flatmate, also in a sequin leotard, dancing around to Kylie Minogue with his boyfriend, Gilly, who is also in a sparkly leotard. I mean – this is not normal life, is it?

"Why don't we just go and do the reading first, and then have a drink afterwards?" I suggest.

"What reading?" asks Dave. "Why are you going to read to Mary? Can't you read or something, Mary?"

"No, she's a psychic, she's going to do a reading for me. I want to find out about Ted and whether we're going to get back together."

"Ah, so that's why you went rushing off," says Juan.

"Ted's a cock," says Dave. "I heard about what happened last night."

Dave hitches his leotard out of his bum in a very undignified manner, and sits on the chair like a cowboy mounting a horse. He has the back of the chair in front of him and his legs either side. In a leotard. No one needs to see that. Sheila seems delighted by the view, judging by the look on her face.

"Let's get going then. How are you feeling, Mary?" she rubs her hand over the crystal ball as she speaks. Sparks fly off it and colours dance across it. It's working now and she's delighted by what she's seeing.

"Oh Mary, Oh Mary," she keeps saying.

I sit in silence, dying to hear what she's got to say.

"Good hands you've got there, Sheila," says Dave. "I love the way you rub the ball."

Sheila gives Dave a cheeky wink and looks like the cat that got the cream. I want to tell her to ignore Dave - he's like that with everyone - but I don't want to burst her bubble. She looks so delighted.

"So, how are you feeling?"

"Like I need a massage from those lovely hands," says Dave.

"Do we have to do this with everyone watching?" I say. "I'd rather it was just you and me. We'll never get anything done like this."

"No, Mary, it's fine. I'm feeling a really good vibe with all these people here watching, it is creating a wonderful atmosphere that is really helping me to get in touch with the spirits that guide you. If you three could all hold hands, and Dave - just move a little bit closer to me and I'm sure I will be able to get a tremendous reading."

Dave needs no more encouragement. He leaps his chair over towards hers and drapes his arm over her shoulder.

Sheila puts her hands over the crystal ball and shuts her

eyes, raising her chin to the ceiling and moving her head around as if she were a puppet being directed from a great puppeteer in the sky. "I'm feeling positive energy, warmth and spiritual healing," she says. "Mary this is really good. I want you to think about the man you want to get back with, and I will read the signs."

Dave raises his hand. "Just a minute - the man you want to get back with? You aren't trying to get back with Fat Ted again, have you? Not after you caught him with really fat Dawn."

"He is crazy," slurs Juan. "He clearly loves Mary but goes out drinking with Dawn."

"So, hang on," Gilly interrupts. "This is the girl who was in the pub with Ted last night? Why does Mary want to get back with him?"

"Please, guys, I'm sitting right in front of you, do you have to have this conversation about me right now, when Sheila is trying to get in touch with my spiritual guides?"

"Sorry," mutters Dave, winking at me. "So, you're single, are you?" I notice him drop his arm from round Sheila's shoulder and look me up and down in that lascivious way he has.

I must not spend tonight with Dave. I must not spend tonight with Dave. I must not spend tonight with Dave. He's gorgeous, and I really want to, but I must not spend tonight with Dave.

"That's odd," says Sheila. "Are you thinking about Ted?"

I had been, but this distraction has forced me to think about Dave.

"Because the only feedback I'm getting at the moment is that it would be a really bad idea to sleep with him tonight. Were you thinking about sleeping with Ted tonight?"

Oh God.

"Sheila, I can't do the reading like this. Either we do it on our own, or we'll just do it another day."

"Okay, gentlemen can you excuse me please," says Sheila. "We'll only be an hour or so, then I'll join you for a drink."

"Make sure you do," says Dave, as the three of them walk off - their hairy, sequin-clad bottoms wriggling away from us.

"Those things must be really uncomfortable," I say to Sheila as she watches them, transfixed.

THE SOUND OF MUSIC

❄

Sheila lays her hands over the crystal ball and I feel my heart lift with joy. I can't wait to hear what's going to happen with Ted.

"You're a lovely person," she says. "You have good people looking after you from the afterlife."

"Do I? What are they saying?"

"They are telling you to relax and that everything will turn out OK in the end."

"Yes, but - what do they mean by the end? Do they mean that I'll get with him when I'm 97?"

Sheila laughs then gives a great big guffaw.

"Your grandad's such a flirt, isn't he? Very lovely. Oh! Your grandma is telling him off now. I don't blame her. 'You tell him, Nel.' Ha ha ha. I can see where you get it from, Mary. They're such fun."

"Nel? How did you know my grandma's name was Nel?"

"I'm a psychic," she says. "It's what I do."

I know she's a psychic, and I know she was right about what the future held last time we spoke, but it still comes as a considerable shock to discover that she knows the name of my grandma.

My first instinct is to think that she's seen something lying around the flat with Nel's name on, but that's ridiculous. My grandma died about 15 years ago. I don't even have pictures of her out.

"What do you want to talk about then?

"Ted."

"What's worrying you? Talk me through what your concerns are and what sort of time period are we talking about? Do you want me to look at the long term and whether you're with him and then more short term?"

"Just short term," I blurt out. "I want to know what's going to happen this week and next week. The future in the long term can take care of itself."

Sheila drifts off into one of her mini trances again, rolling her hands over the crystal ball and swaying gently. She smiles to herself and begins to talk. In the very short term, there will be a problem," she says. "Ted will see you in a new light, only for a short while, but it will be unpleasant, I'm afraid to say. There's a letter. I can see a letter. I don't know whether that's the cause of the problem with Ted or the solution to it. There is a letter.

"I am also seeing a group of people. Is there someone called Veronica?"

"Yes, she is a friend of mine. She knows Ted. She came with me to Amsterdam when we went over there to follow him... Anyway, yes – I know Veronica and she knows Ted. How is she involved? He's not seeing her, is he?"

"No, no, no. I think Veronica has a new boyfriend?"

"Does she? Wow. I should call her; I haven't spoken to her for ages."

"I can see her with her mum. Her mum is very glamorous and quite funny."

"Veronica's very attractive, so it wouldn't surprise me," I say. "But how does this all affect me and Ted?"

Sheila snaps her head back and sits forwards. "That's all I'm getting," she says. "Just those three things – something will happen that's worrying and will make him feel like he sees you in a new light, but you'll get over that and understand it, there is a letter involved and something to do with seeing Veronica. Is this making any sense at all?"

"I'm afraid not. It doesn't make any sense; I wonder what it means. You're not getting anything else then?"

"No. That's a lot. I don't normally get anything like that in such a small time period."

"Right. So, when is this all likely to happen?"

"Well that's why it's amazing that I got so much because my guide is pointing me towards tomorrow. That's all going to happen tomorrow."

"Blimey."

"The feeling I'm getting is that it's all okay. Road bumps on the way, but all okay. Now I think it's time to relax, young lady, and enjoy the evening ahead. I think you should let the future unfold. Something's going to happen that's very positive. Let's go and find those men in the leotards and get them to pour us a drink."

"OK," I say, but I'm all muddled up now. I wonder whether I should go down and meet Ted and talk to him tonight? I had no plans to, but perhaps it would be sensible to go and see him in Shambles like he asked me to?

I'll have a drink first though, and see how I feel later.

We move into the sitting room and chat amiably while we sip our drinks. They want to know all about Sheila and Sheila wants to know all about Dave. I'm sure it's the same everywhere the man goes. His life must be a constant round of female attention and deciding which one of his admirers he wants to sleep with next.

"Let's do shots," says Dave. "I've got a brilliant game. I'll be back in two minutes."

We look at one another while Dave wanders out the flat, then rushes back in again moments later.

"Can I borrow a coat or dressing gown or something? I'd forgotten I'm wearing a leotard."

So, Dave runs off again, this time with my large pale blue dressing gown wrapped over his fancy sequinned body. I can't work out whether he looks more ridiculous in my dressing gown or in the leotard. After about half an hour he comes running back up with carrier bags full of booze, and a very attractive girl who can't be more than about 22 years old.

"Meet Lucy," he says.

"Where have you come from?" asks Sheila. This has clearly ruined all her plans for the evening.

"From down the road," she says, meekly, glancing at me and offering a half-smile. She looks terrified, but I can't help wondering what she was expecting when she accepted a party invitation from a man wearing an old dressing gown and a sequined leotard.

I follow Dave into the kitchen to help unload the bags. "I didn't realise you had a date tonight?" I say.

"I didn't. I just bumped into her in the off-licence."

"You've been to the off-licence, dressed like that?"

"Yes, that's why I needed a dressing gown."

"How did you manage to pick up a very attractive young woman?"

"What can I say, Mary? You've either got it or you haven't."

"Come on then, we are dying to see what this game you've got is all about."

At this point in the evening I am still um-ing and ahh-ing about going down to meet Ted. He says in the messages that he will be in Shambles from 9 pm. It is now seven. I want to have a couple more drinks first, then I might wander down there, just to see what he says.

"Put the television on, will you, Mary," says Dave.

"The television? I thought we were going to play a game."

"Just put it on, and can you get Netflix?"

"Yes, what do you want me to find on it?"

"The Sound of Music."

"The what? Are you drunk?"

"Why do you ask that?"

"Because you're sitting there in a sequined leotard and a fat lady's dressing gown, asking me to put the Sound of Music on the television."

"Good point, but there is a reason for this. Just put it on, woman. Stop complaining."

I find the Sound of Music, as instructed, and begin to play it. Dave instructs me to stop it once the credits have played through, and the film is about to start.

"OK, pause," he says, as the characters are about to appear on screen. This is what we're going to do. We are each going to be a character in the film, and when your character appears, you have to down your drink. If your character sings, you have to do a shot of Sambuca, and if you see stairs, you have to swap drinks with the person to your left. Is that clear?"

I don't think it is clear to any of us, but we agree to give it a go because it sounds really good fun. In fact, it is really good fun. We pick names from a hat (Juan's top hat: we like to do things in style around here). I pick out Lisel, the pretty elder daughter who sings "I am 16 going on 17." I seem to be doing a lot of singing and, therefore, a lot of drinking. We drink and knock back shots and squeal with laughter. The high point (or low point, depending on your view of these games), comes when all the children gather on the stairs to sing good night to their parents and friends, gathered in the house for a party.

Christ almighty. We all have to down our drinks, do a shot, refill our glasses and swap with the person on the left constantly, as the shot drifts off to the faces of those in the party, then moves back to the children on the stairs. Every time the camera goes back to a child, someone has to drink. It is chaos, but enormous fun, and the drunker we get, the funnier everything seems to be as we sing along to the songs, throw drinks down our throats and generally have a brilliant time.

"This is the greatest night of my life," says little Lucy, as she knocks back her Sambuca when Brigitta sings, and giggles into her vodka and tonic.

The rest of it is a bit blurry. Sheila's husband calls her at some point, and she tells him she can't drive back because she's had a drink. Her character comes on screen while she's explaining to him that she wants to stay the night, and there are a lot of shouts of: "It's Gretl...drink, drink, drink" which must really please her poor husband. He tells her she sounds like she'll be in no state to drive back in the morning either, so he'll come and collect her at 8am.

Gretl and Kurt swap drinks and there are squeals of disgust from both of them, as Sheila worms her way into Dave's arms and Lucy looks desperately confused.

While it's all going on, I think of Ted. It's 2.30am and I've no idea where my phone is. I can't even text him to apologise for not turning up. I'll call him in the morning. It will all be fine. I watch Sheila as she lies in Dave's arms, a red feather boa around her neck. I have no idea where that came from or why she's wearing it, but it doesn't matter. Nothing matters. And I drift to sleep, wearing a tutu, all curled up on the sofa with Gilly, as the Sound of Music continues to play on in the background, reminding us all that doe is a female deer and a ray is a drop of golden sun, I smile as Gilly snores. What a lovely night…

AN EARLY MORNING VISIT

❄

God, I feel rough. Where on earth am I? I push cushions off my face and remove the odd headdress that I seem to be wearing. What the hell? My leg is jammed under one of the sofa cushions, and when I pull it out, I see that Gilly is lying on top of me. My head hurts, the floor is sticky and there's a loud banging that is driving me insane. On the armchair, Dave, Lucy and Sheila are all draped in various stages of undress (the women, that is, Dave is still in his sparkly leotard). I've no idea how they managed to sleep like that. Juan is on the floor, sleeping on a huge pile of coats with what look like tea towels on top of him. I'm guessing they were the only things he could find. I don't know. I can't remember anything after *Edelweiss*.

There's still banging at the door. For Christ's sake. Can the postman not just leave whatever it is there, like they did in lockdown. No one needed signatures for everything then. I amble towards the door, stepping over sequins, spilled drink, glasses and empty pizza boxes as I go. When did we get pizza? I glance in the mirror by the door and can't quite believe how bad I look. It's not so much the headdress as the tutu and the cape. When did I dress up? And why? My makeup is smudged all over my face. ALL OVER, and my hair is all standing up on end: matted with alcohol and all knotted from being slept on at a most peculiar angle, with a sofa cushion and a large bloke on top of it. Hopefully the postman won't look too closely.

I open the door to see a familiar man standing there.

The postman? Or a neighbour? I know him from somewhere.

"Hello."

"Hi. I've come to collect Sheila."

"Oh yes, sorry. I thought you had my post. I was confused. Sorry, yes - come in."

"Why did you think I had your post?"

"I thought you were the postman. God my head hurts."

"You came to the house for a reading, didn't you? I remember you. Sheila liked you. She took you to Asda, didn't she? She only ever takes her favourite people to Asda."

"That's right," I say. "You've got a good memory."

"No - I remembered that she liked you when I saw you yesterday. She doesn't like many people, our Sheila. You've done your hair differently. It doesn't look the same as when I saw you yesterday."

I don't really know how to respond to this because my hair is standing completely on end.

"Very modern," he says. "Extremely modern."

"Oh, thank you."

I lead Sheila's husband into the sitting room. If I'd been less drunk and more on the ball, I would have thought to warn Sheila that her husband had arrived. It's not until we are back in the room and he is faced with the sight of three near naked men slumped all over the place wearing leotards, that I realise what a dreadful scene he is being presented with.

"Sheila," I shout, to no avail. "Sheila, wake up."

Sheila sits up and looks at her husband. Her husband looks at Dave, whose crotch is fully on display from his position reclined back against the arm of the chair. Around him is the detritus of a stonking night out, cast across the floor.

"Time to go home," he says. He doesn't sound angry; he sounds hurt by the scene he's seeing. So much worse to hurt him than anger him.

"We were just watching the Sound of Music and playing a drinking game," I explain quickly. "It was all very innocent. You must join us next time."

"Next time?" he says.

"You know what I mean - if we get together in the future, do come."

I decide I should at least cover up Dave's sequinned crotch which seems to be drawing Sheila's husband's eyes to it constantly.

I grab one of the tea towels off Juan just as I hear another voice from the hallway.

"Hello, can I come in?"

Oh God - now the postman is actually here.

"The door's wide open so I'm just coming in, hope that's OK."

Christ, the postman is going to come in and see this ludicrous situation.

Oh no.

It's much worse.

It's Ted.

The love of my life walks into the sitting room to see me laying a tea towel over Dave's exposed crotch in a room full of bodies.

"I'm taking my wife away," Sheila's husband lifts her up to a standing position and assists her as they leave the room.

"I'll return the feather boa very soon," she says to Juan, chortling with laughter. "Thanks for a fab night."

Her sad-looking husband pushes her towards the door, past Ted who just stands there, staring at me.

"I sat in the pub all night," he says. "Praying you'd come. I was worried something had happened, so I thought I'd come and check. Now I can see why you didn't come."

I look at him, blankly.

"I wanted to talk to you. I wanted to sort all this out, but you decide to go to an orgy instead."

I don't have the words to tell him that this is all innocent. It started with me wanting to talk to Sheila about Ted. He's the first thing I think of in the morning and the last thing at night. He means everything to me.

I look down at the ground because I just can't cope with explanations.

"I can't believe you're not even going to talk to me, not going to make me a cup of tea or anything. You just want me to go, don't you?"

"I'll make one," says Gilly, not realising that the cup of tea isn't the issue. Ted doesn't want tea, he wants to be hugged, reassured and made to feel welcome. He feels exactly how I felt when I saw him with Dawn. He wants to be told that everything will be OK. But so do I. I want to be reassured as well. I'm not in the mood for apologising or explaining.

I watch as Ted's eyes follow Gilly into the kitchen. Probably wondering, understandably, why all the men in the room are wearing leotards.

"It's really not like it seems," I say, eventually. "And I decided not to come last night because you have a girlfriend and I don't want to be hurt anymore."

"I haven't got a girlfriend. I've told you so many times - I don't have a girlfriend. What is all this anyway - some great big gang bang?"

"I wish," says a voice from the armchair. Dave lifts his head up.

"Oh Christ it's you. Great!" says Ted.

"We were just having fun. No harm done," says Dave, reaching out for Lucy who is lying so still I fear she might be dead.

"Mary...I don't know what you want me to say, or do. I'm at a loss."

"We just all crashed on the sofas after a few drinks."

"Oh well, I guess that's fine then."

"Well where else was I supposed to go? This place is packed."

"The pub to see me? Your bedroom? Christ, there are two bedrooms in your flat, Mary. Did it not occur to you to go into one of those? This is too much for me. You know how I feel about you. I'm sick of the madness that follows you around everywhere."

He turns to leave as Dave jumps up to stop him. "Don't go. Mary loves you," he says, reaching out to grab him. Dave's words might have had more impact if he hadn't just fallen out of the side of his leotard as he climbed to his feet. Those things aren't designed with male anatomy in mind.

"Whoa, sunshine, you stay right there," says Ted, backing away from him and turning to leave. "I'll see you around, Mary."

LETTER WRITING

We all sit in my sitting room drinking strong coffee and piles of toast in the hope that it will sober us up. The gentlemen have changed out of their sequin leotards (there's a sentence I never thought I'd write!) and poor Lucy, who doesn't know what is going on, has headed off home, with a promise from Dave that he will call her really soon. Since I had to remind him of her name four times last night, this seemed very unlikely.

"What now then?" I ask Juan, as I stare at the pizza boxes which are still lying around on the floor. I can't face picking them up and disposing of them just yet.

"What now then, in what way?"

"I mean the whole Ted thing. It feels like it's destined not to work, doesn't it? I mean – really, what on earth are the chances of him rocking up here just as we are emerging from a massive drinking session?"

"To be fair, the chances are pretty high. Most mornings we are emerging from a drunken night."

I want to laugh, but don't feel like anything is remotely funny at the moment. Perhaps, in the fullness of time, I'll look back on this bizarre scene that Ted was confronted with, and think it amusing. Not now though. Now I just feel sad. "But there aren't that many mornings when we wake up with all the men wearing sequin leotards, and angry husbands collecting their psychic wives. I mean, I know we're a bit mad, but we're not usually *that* mad."

"Good point," says Gilly. "You're going to have to explain it all to him."

"I can't bear it. If I go round there now, he'll just stand there with his arms folded looking all hurt and cross. I know I'm a complete idiot. But that was all perfectly innocent. Him being out with Dawn is much worse."

"And he offered to explain that to you," says Juan, swinging his legs and almost sending his cup of coffee flying across the floor. "Now you need to do the same. Go and have a shower, get dressed and look as good as you can, and go round there now. I'll clean this place up and it will be spotless by the time you get back and I will have a nice lunch on the table and we'll have a relaxing afternoon in front of Netflix. How does that sound?"

"It all sounds brilliant apart from me going to explain myself to Ted. Can we miss that bit out?"

"You can miss that bit out if you don't want to get back with him... But since that's what you want more than anything on God's earth, I suggest you go round there and explain why you had three men in sequin leotards draped across your sitting room first thing this morning."

Gilly chuckles and shakes his head. "You've got to see the

funny side of it," he says, before looking up at my sad face and realising that I am not quite seeing the funny side of anything at the moment.

"I'm going to have a bath," I say. "That will give me some thinking time. I'll go round there in an hour, and if the offer of you tidying up the flat and making me lunch still stands, that would be wonderful."

"The offer still stands," says Juan.

Relaxing in the bath, with bubbles up to my neck, things start to feel a little more positive. I even start to see the funny side of the incident that just happened... just. The whole notion of having to go round to explain to the man you love why he was confronted by such a weird tableau in the early hours of this morning is something that just doesn't seem to happen to other people.

I pull myself out of the water, wash my hair and have a shower. I've got a bit of a thing about washing my hair in the bath water. I'm convinced it will never be properly clean that way. Then I go into my bedroom, and make a decision to write everything down, so I can read a speech, rather than trying to amble my way through a ridiculous apology while my head feels like it's caught in a vice.

Dear Ted,

I love you. I've always loved you.
    I can't remember a time before you were in my life.

You bring colour, magic, music and joy every day we're together. The time we have been apart has been heart-breaking. I can't tell you how much I've missed you, and how much I've wanted you back. You turning up this morning has made me think that you have feelings for me, and maybe we do have a chance to make it work.

On the subject of this morning... I'm not really sure what to say... we got drunk, ordered pizza, and fell asleep in the sitting room. It had been a really fun night, and – yes, of course I should have gone to my bedroom – but we were having so much fun but I didn't want to leave the party. You know what I'm like. I like to stay at the party and drink the last few drops of it up.

I don't feel like I owe you an explanation, because we're not going out together, but I'm doing it because I love you, I want to be with you, and it's frustrating the hell out of me that things keep happening to keep us apart.

I don't know what else to say. Mary x

I read back over the letter and it brings tears to my eyes. It's perfect. I need to write more when I've got a hangover, it reads so much better than when I write sober.

"I'm off," I shout into the sitting room, where Gilly and Juan, true to their word, are busy tidying up, while Dave lounges on the sofa.

"Want a lift?" he asks.

"You can't drive, you were drinking till about an hour ago."

"I'm fine, I stopped drinking quite early and just lay there watching you lot getting hammered."

"Really? Gosh, that would be great, if you're absolutely sure."

"Absolutely. Anything to get away from these two little cleaning fairies disturbing my peace."

He winks at Juan as he clambers off the sofa and grabs his keys. "I'll be back soon," he says as the two of us walk towards the door.

Behind us I can hear Juan say to Gilly: "I quite like the idea of being a cleaning fairy."

It takes us about half an hour to do the 10-minute drive to Ted's house because Dave keeps turning the wrong way. In fairness. I keep forgetting to tell him he has to turn. All in all, there's no doubt that I could've walked there quicker.

"Do you want me to wait in the car while you go to talk to him?"

"No, honestly, don't worry – you head home and I'll meet you back there soon."

"Okay, babes. It's probably better for me to get off the road anyway."

"Why?"

"Because I'm absolutely hammered."

"You told me you stopped drinking hours ago."

"Yes, I said that so you get in the car. Of course I didn't stop drinking hours ago, I haven't quite stopped drinking yet."

"Oh my God, Dave, go straight home and don't get in the car again today."

Dave laughs at me, then lurches into the wrong gear and stalls. Then there's a bit of revving and a sudden shriek as he zooms off up the road. It's like he's never driven a car before. I hate that I got into the car with him. What was I thinking?

I walk up to Ted's flat, but can see straight away that his car isn't there. Damn. For some reason it hadn't occurred to me that he would've gone anywhere. I assumed he just got cross in my flat and stormed home.

For a fleeting second, I reach into my bag to get my phone to ask Dave to turn round and come back and pick me up. But then I stop myself for two good reasons – firstly Dave was very drunk, and needs to get out of the car and not come back and pick me up. Secondly, annoyingly, I have left my handbag in the car so I don't have a phone with which to call anyone.

The day is getting worse as it progresses. All I have in my hands is my speech. I try the door but there is no answer. I read through my speech, and wonder whether I should just push that through the front door? Or should I go home, and try again later, so I can see him face-to-face?

I think of the letter arriving on the floor and one of those people who live in the flats below, picking it up and reading it. I don't have a pen on me so I can't write his name on the outside, where it is folded over, or write "private" or anything, so I push the letter back into my pocket and head off back down the path onto the street.

The walk home does me a bit of good, to be honest. Fresh air and thinking time have lifted my mood. I'm annoyed that I keep getting myself into these extraordinary situations, but then so does Ted. He was the one on a date the night before last. And we got into some pretty extraordinary situations when we were seeing one another. Like the time we had to hide under the table in the bar in Fulham because his workmates were in there, and he had taken the day off sick to be with me. We ate a whole meal under the table, with the staff bringing us cutlery and condiments and placing them on the concrete while we tried to act as if it was the most normal thing in the world.

Yeah, Ted is the sort of guy that attracts drama too. It's not just me.

Last night was insane. The really daft thing is that if Ted had been there, he would've loved it. He wouldn't have fitted into the sequined leotards, so he might have had to forego that part of the evening, but he would definitely have been up for the drink along to The Sound of Music.

I pull my phone out of my pocket to ring Sheila, and check she's OK.

She answers on the first ring. "How are you doing?" I say.

"Oh my God, I think I'm still drunk. What an incredible night, though. I had a brilliant time. Thanks so much for inviting me, Mary."

I wasn't aware of having invited her as such, but – there we go.

"You and Dave seemed to be getting on well," I say.

"I know, hang on," she says, as I hear her scurry out of the room and up the stairs, presumably away from her husband so she can talk to me properly.

"He's so gorgeous, Mary. I really like him. My husband and I just haven't been getting on with each other... Not for years, if I'm honest. We are different people. Being with Dave last night made me realise that I could do much better for myself."

"Hang on, hang on... When you say 'being with Dave' what do you mean? Don't listen to a word the guy says. He's got girls dotted all around the place, and will never be faithful to anyone. Please don't even think about throwing away your marriage based on anything Dave might have said or done."

"I think he might be the one."

"He was the one for last night, Sheila. Honestly, you have to believe the man is not going to commit, you'll just get hurt. Stay with your husband, see whether you can work it out, and if you can't and want to separate from him, do that. But keep away from Dave."

"Well let's see shall we, he said he'll ring me, let's see if he does."

"Indeed," I say. "I hope he does; I'm not trying to be mean or anything, but I don't want you to get hurt, And I've seen many, many girls crying outside the flat. I see different girls going in and out of there all the time."

"That was all before he met me," says Sheila.

I explain to her about this morning's activities with Ted, and how I have been round there with a letter, but not left it for him.

"Mary, don't you see... It's what I predicted. It's an incident that changed his view of you."

"Oh my God, of course. And then there was a letter, and I've written him a letter. Oh my God, Sheila, this is all amazing."

"Let's talk soon and I'll let you know if there are any developments on the Dave front. If you bump into him, say lots of nice things about me, won't you."

I walk down the road towards my flat, thinking about the whole situation with Sheila. There is no doubt that she has psychic tendencies, and can see into the future, which poses the question, why on earth would she think that there was any sort of future for her and Dave? Whatever happened between them in the night, which judging by what Sheila said was 'something', Dave isn't the type to follow up with a phone call and future dates. If she is psychic, why can't she see that? And, without being cruel, Sheila must be mid-30s, I don't think I've ever seen Dave with anyone over 21. Sheila is not unattractive, but she is certainly not gorgeous like all these women Dave goes for. I really hope she doesn't get hurt. I might warn him not to hurt her.

When I arrive at the flat, the door is wide open. I shout out to Juan and Gilly. "He wasn't there, I couldn't talk to him, and I didn't put a note through the door because it's a shared hallway and someone else would have read it. I…"

"Oh, hi Ted."

"I came back here to talk to you," he says "I shouldn't have rushed off like that."

"I can kind of understand why you did though," I say. I look around the room to see that Gilly and Juan have tidied it up completely. It's like the scene from earlier in the day had never happened.

"I wrote this."

I pass the note to him, and watch him open it.

"Don't read it now," I say. "Read it when you get home."

"I'm so sorry," says Ted. "I'm such a rational guy normally, but around you I seem to be more judgemental than Simon Cowell."

I laughed at this. He smiled too.

"What do you fancy – shall we meet up for a drink or something? Unless this letter tells me that you never want to see me again."

"The letter doesn't say that, and I'd love to meet for a drink."

"Tomorrow night?"

"I should be able to do that."

"How about if I pick you up at 7:30? I'll think of somewhere nice for us to go."

"That would be great. Nice to see you guys," he says in the direction of Juan and Gilly. "You both look much better without those ridiculous leotards on."

At the front door he turns to me and hugs me again, kissing me lightly on the cheek. "I'll see you tomorrow night, okay. Nothing is allowed to go wrong."

"And read the letter," I say, as I watch him walk down the steps before closing the door behind him.

UNWELCOME GUESTS

"WHAT AM I GOING TO WEAR?" I scream at Charlie. "We're meeting tomorrow night and I have nothing appropriate."

"Are you telling me you want to go back to Zara?"

"Yeah, great idea. I could pick up that beigey grey tent dress."

"You could do that, but I can't guarantee that Ted will be swept off his feet if you do. Anyway, didn't you say before that you want to keep things casual and don't want to get all dressed up."

"Yeah, I know, but I just want a nice top to wear with my white three-quarter length trousers. I've ordered this bright green top but I'm convinced it won't get here in time, and if it doesn't, what then? I'm waffling now, aren't I? Jabbering away because I'm excited. Sorry!"

"No need to apologise, I'm delighted to see you like this. Just make sure that you have a proper chat to Ted tomorrow night. Don't get drunk. You need to find out exactly what's been going on with Dawn. You need to get everything cleared up. All cards on the table."

The parcel arrived at around midday the next day, and the postman was treated to a huge squeal of delight as I grabbed it off him and ran into my bedroom. It's always a challenge ordering things online, and hoping they will fit and look as good on you as they do on the incredibly skinny, young models they use. When we were in lockdown, I became obsessed with ordering things because I was so bored, and so sad about everything happening with Ted, so I wanted to cheer myself up with parcels. They arrived, I tried the things on, looked ridiculous in them, and sent them straight back. It kept me busy and it kept the Royal Mail and various courier companies on their toes for about six weeks.

This time, I'm delighted to say, there will be no need for the top to be returned. It looks stunning. It's got tiny little sequins on the pockets. I know that sounds a bit naff, now I say it out loud, but it is loose and flowing and in this lovely bright green colour which seems to go nicely with my hair (my hair isn't green, you understand, but somehow the bright green goes well with my blonde hair), by the time I put my fake tan on later and do my make up nicely, I will look exactly like Charlize Theron or someone like that.

By 7 o'clock I'm ready, though not looking at all like Charlize Theron or any other major movie star, and walk into the sitting room to be greeted by wolf whistles from Juan and Gilly.

"Why thank you, kind sirs," I say.

"You look properly gorgeous," says Juan. "Is that top new,

the colour really suits you. You should definitely wear bright colours a lot more."

"I know, everyone says that, and I think this colour particularly suits me, but I'm always reluctant to wear green, because my uniform is green and I have to wear that all day."

"Yes, but this is a whole different level of green from the Kermit outfit. You look amazing, you gorgeous girl. Have a great time, won't you?"

"I will, thank you."

"Do you want a glass before you go?" asks Gilly, raising a bottle of Sauvignon Blanc that he and Juan have clearly started.

"You know...I won't. I really don't want to be drunk by the time I get there, and Ted is picking me up, so he won't be drinking. Would be a really good idea if I wasn't smashed by 8 o'clock."

"Fair enough, not a bad decision," says Juan. "What time is Ted coming?"

"He is due here at 7:30."

"I bet he is here already. It's 7:10, he'll want to make sure he's here on time. I bet you anything he is sitting in his car outside."

I'm not sure whether Gilly is right, so I creep up to the window to check, just in case. And there is Ted, sitting in the driver's seat, completely unaware that he is being observed, as he plays with his phone.

"Well that's definitely a good sign. The man is keen."

We pretend that we don't realise that Ted has been sitting outside, when he knocks on the door at about 7:27, looking smart in a blue blazer, instead of his usual jeans and T-shirt. He has shaved and I can see the red rising on his face where he has been rather rough with the razor. I know the man so well.

We walk to his car and he opens the door for me. I look up at the flat and see the curtains twitch. I knew those two would be watching.

"I've had an idea, why don't we go to the pub we used to go to when we first met?" he says.

"Which pub? What do you mean?"

"Oh, how quickly you forget. The one next to the fat club. Do you remember? A group of us used to go down there after the sessions and have a few beers. Please tell me that you remember because it was the highlight of my life every week for the whole time we went there. I fancied you like mad, but I didn't know how to get you to notice me. You just didn't seem remotely interested."

"Ha ha. I like to keep my cards close to my chest. Yes, let's go there. That's a lovely idea. It'll be fun."

"By the way, the letter you sent made me cry."

I lean over and rest my hand on his leg, like the old times, then I pull it back again because we're not quite at 'old times' yet, and I feel a bit silly.

It's very strange walking into the pub again after so long. The courses I did at the community centre a few doors down really changed my life. They introduced me to a whole new group of people, and though I've been a bit useless at keeping in touch with them through lockdown, I know they'll always be in my life. I also lost around 30lbs while on the courses, which is pretty good going. Then I gained a 280lb lump in Ted. The best benefit of all.

He pushes the door open and stands back to allow me to go

through first, and it reminds me of how he always did that, always so gentlemanly and thoughtful.

"What do you fancy to drink?" he says.

"I'll just have a diet coke please."

"Really? Are you sure you don't fancy wine?"

"No, you're not drinking, so neither will I. Let's just both stay sober and have a nice chat."

"We are sounding very middle-aged," he says, as he orders two diet cokes and we wander over to a corner table. We sit down, look at one another, and he smiles. "It's really lovely to see you."

I smile back. "We're hopeless aren't we, Ted."

"Yep."

"Can I just tell you what's been happening from my point of view?"

"Of course," he says.

"Well - when we were apart, I missed you so much. I just couldn't wait to see you. We worked out that Charlie's birthday was in six weeks, so I went on a Six Week Transformation diet to look as good as possible. I even went on a trip to Italy as part of it, organised by Dawn. Then when I was on the trip, Dawn told me that you and she were going out together."

"What?"

"She phoned me in Italy to tell me."

"It was nothing like that," said Ted. "Honestly. Why would she say that? Is this the trip to Italy that you went on with Roberto?"

"Who's Roberto?"

"OK. Look - let me tell you everything. My sister wants to do a blog and asked me whether I knew anyone who did one. I mentioned the stuff you'd done with Dawn and she took a look, then she asked me whether she could meet Dawn. I fixed up for them to meet for a drink and I went too. She called a couple of times afterwards and said she had some notes and things. I met her a couple of times to collect things from her. She was really kind and helpful. I got the impression that she quite liked me, but nothing was ever said. Then she told me that she'd arranged for you to go to Italy with your boyfriend Roberto."

"She's such a cow."

"I don't know - she seemed to be friendly and helpful. Perhaps she got the wrong end of the stick about Roberto. Was there a Roberto on your trip?"

"No. Ted, honestly, she just made it up. I hate her. Why did you see her last night?"

"She's given my sister a free holiday to write about for the blog, now that lockdown has lifted. I met her last night to pick up the tickets and sort everything out with her. It felt really awkward when you came in, because you'd mentioned her at the party and I didn't really know why. I get it now though."

"Ted, I'm sure she was being really nice to your sister, but she definitely fancies you. She told me that she was seeing you. Why would she do that?"

"I don't know. Are you sure you didn't just misinterpret what she said?"

"No Ted - I'm not deaf."

"But you did jump to the conclusion that I was with her in Kingston and I wasn't."

"Yes, I jumped to conclusions *because* she said she was going out with you. And, another thing...Dave saw you kissing her. What was all that about?"

"Well I never. What are the chances?" says a voice from the

other side of the bar. "I haven't seen you guys for so long, how are you?"

It's Veronica who rushes over to hug me before hugging Ted. She is with a very glamorous older woman. "Have you met my mum, Kat?" she says.

Ted stands up and kisses her mum on the cheek, before Kat and Veronica sit down at the table.

"You don't mind if we join you, do you?" says Veronica. "I'm not interrupting a romantic night, out am I?"

"No," we say, in unison, even though this is the worst possible timing. I desperately want to talk to Ted.

"What do you do, Kat?" asks Ted, out of politeness rather than any real interest.

"I work as a fashion adviser and personal shopper," she says. "I work mainly with older women because I swear to God it can be hard to find nice clothes when you're older. I turned 50 a couple of weeks ago and trying to find funky, modern and fashionable clothing that doesn't make you look like mutton dressed as lamb is impossible when you're my age. So, women come to me, and we gossip, have a glass of champagne and find them the best clothes possible."

"You look really lovely," I say, and she really does. Veronica is very beautiful, but her mum is spectacularly attractive, I bet she used to be a supermodel when she was younger. She's got blonde hair and lovely blue eyes, perfect skin with hardly a wrinkle in sight (Botox alert!) and her clothes are beautiful. You can tell they are expensive and well looked after. She is extraordinarily slim and dresses like a Parisian, with three quarter length black trousers and a black jacket with this cream ruffled shirt underneath and a beret. Her jewellery is beautiful too: gold necklaces and lovely gold earrings. She has more make-up on her face than I have in my makeup bag, but somehow it seems to suit her.

"So, what do you do, Ted?" she asks.

"I'm afraid it's all very dull. I work for a company that provides equipment and computers to the NHS, and I have to go and do deals. I'm kind of in procurement but I do the big financial deals so I'm officially a director of the company."

"Wow, that's really impressive," says Kat. "You look like the sort of sophisticated man who would be doing a big important job like that."

"Thank you," says Ted, blushing a little. Kat really is very beautiful and just a little flirty. "I'm afraid I'm neither sophisticated nor important, but I do appreciate the compliment..."

"Do my eyes betray me, or is that the lovely Mary Brown?" says another familiar voice. It's Liz, the lady who led the weight loss course. She hugs me closely before sitting down next to Ted and asking him how he'd been.

"The last time I saw your lovely lady, I was in Tesco's doing the weekly shop and she was buying an absurd amount of cake."

"Oh yes," I say. "That was for the 'World Cup of Cakes' that I ran during lockdown."

"And then I saw you chatting to a potato."

"Yes, well lockdown was a difficult time," I say, as Ted looks at me quizzically. "I saw the potato lying there in the street, and it seemed so lonely."

"You really are bonkers," says Ted.

After about four Diet Cokes, and realising that, as much fun as Kat, Liz and Veronica are, we aren't going to get any time to ourselves to talk here, which was the main point of the evening, Ted and I make our excuses and leave.

"We must all meet up again soon," says Kat, as we pick up our coats. "I'll bring a top that will look perfect on you, Mary."

"Oh, thank you," I say.

"As long as you don't bring any of your boyfriends, mum," says Veronica.

"You don't like your mum's boyfriend?"

"I am dead against them because most of them are younger than me," says Veronica, as Ted and I burst out laughing.

"You've got a toy boy!" I say.

"Well all the guys my own age are either dead or looking for a carer. Becoming a cougar is the best way forward."

"Mum's best friend is also going out with a younger man, they go out in a foursome, and it looks like mums taking the boys out for something to eat after football practice."

Veronica says it with such affection that we all laugh along, and Kat hugs her daughter tightly. "You wait, my dear," she says. "Wait till you turn 50 and let's see how you feel about it."

Ted and I get into the car, and smile at one another. "So much for our romantic night," he says. "I suppose it's my fault for choosing that pub."

"Yes I know, I was so disappointed when they came over and joined us, but Kat is hysterical, isn't she? Such a funny woman. I loved her."

"Yes she was, and she looked incredible for her age."

"Yes. She's really beautiful."

"But not as beautiful as you, Mary."

He leans over and kisses me gently on the cheek. "Let's get you home."

"Yes," I say, "Let's go home."

We pull up outside my flat and he kisses me gently on the cheek. I think he's going to turn my face towards him so he can kiss me on the mouth but he doesn't. He sits back in his seat. "You have to laugh, don't you?"

"I guess so," I say, then I add, nervously: "Look. Do you want to come in?"

"No, I better get off," he says quickly. "But let's meet soon."

I'm so deflated as I walk through my front door that I don't even turn and wave goodbye to him. It has been a lovely night despite us not being able to spend much time alone together, but at the end there it was if we were friends and he was dropping me off like one of his mates. It didn't feel like the end of a date. Perhaps he just wants to be friends with me? By the time I walk into the sitting room and flop onto the sofa next to Juan and Gilly, I'm almost in tears.

"Whoah. Glass of wine?" asks Juan.

"A large one please."

I walk into the kitchen after Juan and take a big gulp of wine before saying anything. Then there's a loud knock at the door.

"Pizza!" declares Gilly, jumping up.

"Oh good," I say. "I'm afraid I'm going to change out of this top and help myself to a piece."

But when Gilly walks back in, he's not with pizza, he's with Ted.

"Can I change my mind?" he says.

"About what?"

"About coming in."

"Of course."

"I thought that leaving was the right thing to do, but I want to be with you, Mary. I don't want to play games."

"Me neither."

"When I talked to the boys about us, and how much I love you, they told me to take it easy. They said I'd scare you off if I came on too strongly. Except Henry - he had no valuable advice, he just kept insisting that you jumped onto the front of his boat, but he's nuts."

"Oh yes - completely nuts."

"Then I was going to drive away and I thought 'what am I doing?' I'm fed up of worrying about what's the right thing to do and what's the wrong thing to do.

"I love you Mary. I've loved you since we first met, and I can't imagine ever not loving you. I want to be with you forever. Can we just forget the past few months ever happened and carry on having a lovely time together?"

"I'd like that more than anything in the world."

"So, Mary Brown. Will you be my girlfriend?"

"I will."

"I think we're going to need more pizza and a lot more wine," says Gilly, opening the fridge and pulling out the champagne that we save for special occasions. "Lovely to see you two back together again."

And I look at Ted, and all the tears that had stored in the back of my eyes earlier come tumbling out. But this time they are tears of joy.

"I love you, Ted."

"Love you too, Mary Brown."

ends

THE MYSTERIOUS MANHUNT is out in November! The follow-up to Mysterious Invitation will explore what happens when Mary catches up with all of the characters from Mysterious Invitation, as they travel to find the Gower family and learn more about the man they had never heard of, who gathered them at his funeral. Only this time, Ted might go too…but only if he can explain to Mary why he was kissing Dawn.

Or, if you can't wait till then, the first ever Handbook for Adorable Fat Girls is out on 1st August.

Thank you so much BBx

Printed in Great Britain
by Amazon